MOONLIGHT COCKTAIL

MOONLIGHT COCKTAIL

A JACK SULLIVAN NOVEL

WILLIAM CASSIDY

DISCUS BOOKS
ALEXANDRIA, VIRGINIA

ISBN: 978-1-7337346-2-2 (paperback)

PROLOGUE

Nervously skimming the old books, trying to avoid being noticed by others in the library, the Reader searched through descriptions of ancient Hawaiian rites. Enough noise was generated by the rattling pages that those at nearby tables looked up from their own books and scowled. The Reader immediately stopped and stared at the open pages, waited five minutes, then began to turn them again, slowly this time.

After four hours, the Reader found the object of the search, opened a notebook, and began writing with a hand that shook so violently the words were barely legible. Looking around, convinced that others were watching, the Reader got up and left the library.

All that remained now was to ask the right questions of the right person. It would be easy now. With a local telephone book, the search could begin. Thereafter, it would only be a matter of waiting for the right opportunity.

The Reader left the library, signing out more quickly than signing in, relieved to be away from the Bishop Museum's reading room and the skeptical eyes of legitimate researchers. The Honolulu phone book listed several Herbal Medicine practitioners who might know where to find what the Reader was looking for.

The next day, concocting a phony medical problem as the reason for the calls, the Reader asked each practitioner whether the object of the search could be found on Oahu. After speaking to one who knew its location, the Reader purchased the necessary tools to remove it from the field where it grew wild — and toxic enough to kill a man.

CHAPTER ONE

The pitch of the airliner's engines suddenly deepened as they slowed down over the Central Pacific Ocean, one hundred miles east of the Hawaiian Islands. As Jack Sullivan awakened, the pilot announced their descent into Honolulu International Airport; they would arrive in twenty minutes. Jack raised the window screen and gazed down at the Pacific, fifteen thousand feet below.

Whitecaps splashed the ocean's deep blue surface like stars lighting up a night sky. Soon the color of the sea would lighten from the cobalt blue of the deep Pacific to royal blue when the islands came into view and then to aquamarine as the aircraft flew over the reefs surrounding Oahu. But these changes would not be gradual. There is no continental shelf extending far into the Pacific from the Hawaiian Islands. These volcanic islands rise abruptly out of the ocean, and the surrounding sea turns dark a mere two miles offshore.

Jack was returning from meetings in San Francisco with coffee brokers who were interested in buying the Kona coffee beans grown on his plantation on the Big Island of Hawaii. He was eager to get back to Honolulu, where he and Katherine lived most of the week. Ten minutes later, the Hawaiian Islands appeared on the left side of the aircraft; soon Jack could make out Pearl Harbor, the Waikiki Beach hotels, and Diamond Head crater on the southwest side of the island of Oahu. As the plane touched

1

down, Jack bundled his newspapers and magazines, jammed them into his briefcase, and grabbed his cell phone. It was just after six in the morning, but he wanted to hear his wife's voice.

"Hello", Katherine's sleepy voice responded after the second ring.

"I'm home, baby. Want to have breakfast with Hawaii's newest coffee farmer?"

"I'd love to but it has to be quick. I have a very good customer coming into my shop at seven-thirty to pick up a dress before her plane leaves for Tokyo."

"That's all right. I'll go down to the Club after breakfast and work out to make up for the two days I spent sitting on my ass in the City of Saint Francis. See you in twenty minutes."

The airport wasn't crowded, and Jack made good time getting to the Royal Hawaiian Hotel in Waikiki. Katherine was waiting at the door of their suite wearing a floral sundress and high heels, her blond hair pulled back in a pony tail with a fresh gardenia set in the band.

"Welcome home, hubby," Katherine exclaimed with a smile.

I missed you, baby," Jack replied as he embraced her. "Very nice dress," he said as his eyes took in his young wife.

"Well, thank you, Jack. We can only hope that my customers like it too. It's my latest design, and they can have one too, for the right price," Katherine said as she led Jack out to their lanai.

After another long embrace, they sat down to papaya juice and coffee. Jack regaled his wife with tales of his negotiations with the coffee brokers in San Francisco, and Katherine responded with stories of the various characters who had visited her dress shop while Jack was gone.

Suddenly she gasped. "Jack, it's seven-fifteen, I've got to run. Let's do something fun tonight," she called as she dashed out the door.

"I promise. I'll call you as soon as I make a plan."

Jack walked to the kitchen phone, called the concierge, and asked for his car to be brought up to the front entrance of the hotel.

Ten minutes later, he was in his blue Jeep Wrangler, zigzagging from the hotel's driveway to Kalakaua Avenue, the main street along Waikiki Beach. He drove east toward Diamond Head, past the Moana Surfrider Hotel and then the statue of Duke Kahanamoku, the father of modern surfing, in front of Kuhio Beach.

Jack always enjoyed the ten-minute ride from the Royal Hawaiian to Diamond Head. He had first driven this stretch of Kalakaua Avenue twenty years earlier when he was a Naval Officer serving on a Destroyer based at Pearl Harbor and he still got a kick out of it.

Jack was on his way to the Diamond Head Canoe Club where, for the last two months, he'd been working out every other day by paddling his one-man outrigger canoe along the several-mile length of Waikiki Beach. He smiled with satisfaction as he passed Queen Kapiolani Park on his left. It was two miles around the park, and he could run around it twice in 36 minutes. Not bad for a forty-five year old guy.

Jack could already feel the sun beginning to warm his face as he passed the World War I Memorial Natatorium on the beach to his right. The tradewinds out of the northeast were gentle, and the Pacific Ocean looked calm when he passed the New Otani Hotel, located on the site where, local legend has it, Robert Louis Stevenson penned *Treasure Island* under a hau tree. Farther along, just past the entrance to the Surf Hotel on the eastern end of Waikiki, Jack turned into the driveway of the Diamond Head Canoe Club. A two-level building with gray coral stone walls outside and koa and mahogany inside, it was open to the elements on two sides and reminded Jack of houses designed by Frank Lloyd Wright. His favorite room was the Lanai, with its roof formed by the branches of hau trees that laced their way through an overhead trellis.

The Club sat on the beach at the foot of the Diamond Head crater, two miles west of the Diamond Head Lighthouse. Jack had taken up paddling shortly after he was admitted to the Diamond Head. It reminded him of the old days in yacht clubs on the east coast where he had grown up, clubs you joined primarily to race sailboats and drink and gossip at the bar. But here the drinks were usually Mai Tai's rather than Martini's. To correct this imbalance, Jack had introduced his friends at the Diamond Head to the special martini he had concocted and named the "Wiki Wiki," which means speedy in Hawaiian. It called for two shots of Tito's Vodka to be shaken thoroughly in an ice-filled cocktail shaker and then poured into a chilled Martini glass. Instead of vermouth, one capful of Tanqueray Gin was then poured on top of the ice shavings that floated on the vodka, followed by a twist of lemon and olives on the side. Jack told his friends that this crystal clear libation instantly improved his personality, and they unanimously agreed. It rapidly improved theirs as well.

Jack waved to the Club Manager, Noa Watson, as he walked through the Club's lobby to the Men's Locker Room. Noa returned the wave and asked him to stop by after he finished paddling. Jack then heard a familiar voice booming from the direction of the scale at the far corner of the locker room. The greeting had been launched from the hawk-like face that topped a powerful six-foot frame and peered out at the world from beneath a bald pate, exultant in the confirmation that, even after forty years, his weight remained within five pounds of his college days at the University of Southern California. The voice was that of Gordon Grant – local real estate magnate, President of the Diamond Head Canoe Club, Navy veteran, and Jack's good friend and paddling coach.

"Sullivan, you're not here to practice paddling so you can compete with me, are you?" Grant barked, barely able to conceal the smile on his face. "That would be ludicrous and embarrassing if it got out to the Club. It could even affect your standing among members. No, I'm sure you're here to take a steam or a sauna followed by a nice warm shower. Isn't that what east coast lawyers do at athletic clubs? Take 'executive workouts'?"

"Grant, you are completely full of shit. How does your wife put up with you?"

"Put up with me? She adores me! You haven't yet learned the mystery of these islands, have you Sullivan? Well, as with everything else since you arrived in this paradise six months ago, I will have to teach you."

"Thank you, Professor," Jack said with a smile.

"You're welcome," Grant nodded in mock seriousness. "Now, how far are you paddling this morning?"

"I thought I'd go down to the Ala Wai Boat Harbor and back. You know, a relaxing two-hour cruise along Waikiki."

"Excellent!" Grant pronounced. "I just did that myself. Of course, I got up earlier than you did and now I'm ready to start the capitalist phase of my day."

"My turn comes later, Gordo. I just got in from the mainland," Jack called as he left the locker room and walked toward the storage racks where he kept his canoe.

"Hey Jack," Grant called, "the Diva and I want to have dinner with you and Katherine this week. Georgia reminded me that your wife keeps beating me at Dominoes, so now I've got to show her I've just been going easy on Katherine because you guys are new to Hawaii."

"We'd love to, but, if my recollection serves me correctly, my wife has been routinely kicking your ass at Five Up fair and square," Jack laughed as he headed toward the beach with his canoe.

The Pacific could not have been more inviting. There was barely a ripple on the surface, even at the reef thirty yards offshore. Jack slid his white carbon fiber canoe into the water, pushed it out a few yards beyond the wavelets that lapped at the shore, and jumped on board, straddling it until he gained his balance. Unlike a traditional outrigger canoe, you sat on this canoe rather than in it, almost like sitting on top of a surfboard. Typical of the one-man canoes raced at the Club, Jack's canoe was twenty-three feet long, and there was an area two-thirds of the way back shaped like a scallop that served as the seat. He brought his long legs, one at a time, on board the main hull and extended them until his feet rested on the pedals that steered the canoe, dipped his black paddle into the Pacific and took long slow strokes on the left side of the main hull, through the azure water that passed under the canoe and the aluminum outriggers connecting that hull to a smaller hull called an ama. His left foot nudged the pedal to turn the canoe slightly left toward the opening in the reef that protected the beach shared by the Diamond Head Canoe Club and the Surf Hotel. As he reached forward with his shoulders and arms to extend the paddle, he felt the canoe begin to move through the water swiftly, more like a glider in flight than a boat.

On Jack's right, a black rock jetty extended twenty-five yards from the beach. As he reached the end of the jetty, he looked to his left and spotted the orange windsock on top of the black stake thirty feet away. The windsock and the seaward tip of the jetty marked either side of a break in the reef that allowed canoes to slip through to the open sea. Jack always took notice of these marks as he left the security of the beach area, because it was not easy to see them when returning. And if the wind increased and the swells and waves grew higher, it would be even more important to find the channel opening so the waves didn't pound the canoe, and its occupant, on the coral reef.

As Jack cruised through the opening in the reef, he felt the Pacific beneath him rise. No matter how calm the ocean seemed from the beach and no matter how small the waves appeared from that vantage point, there was almost always a significant swell at the reef. And it looked and felt mountainous when sitting on a small canoe three inches above the surface of the water. Jack jabbed his paddle deeper into the blue water, increased the rate of his strokes, and propelled the canoe clear of the reef. Then the Pacific was flat again, almost like an inland lake, but deeper now, a darker blue and mysterious.

Shortly after he began paddling at the Club, Jack learned that the locals don't like to tell tourists too much about the water beyond the reef. They think it's bad for business and they're probably right, because beyond the reef lies the unconstrained expanse of the Pacific Ocean and all the creatures that call it home. In the middle of this vast ocean, the Hawaiian Islands are sometimes called the most remote spot in the world because they are farther from any continent than any other place on earth. Jack thought this assessment was a bit extreme but he conceded that, technically speaking, the Hawaiian Islands were indeed remote, and the presence of creatures like Tiger Sharks and Reef Sharks a short distance offshore was evidence of the sometimes hostile environment that surrounded these otherwise peaceful islands.

As Jack paddled west toward the curving line of Waikiki hotels, he saw a U.S. Navy Destroyer heading toward him from Pearl Harbor, probably bound for the Navy's operating area ten miles off Diamond Head, where it would conduct antisubmarine warfare training exercises. The sight of the sleek gray hull with its high bow, sweeping sheerline, and raked mast reminded Jack of his own years on an earlier version of this warship. In a flash, it was all there before him – the acrid smell of burning fuel oil mixing with the pungent salt air of the open sea; the sound of the ocean hissing past the hull; sharp voices articulating the age-old commands that navigate ships out of harbors; visiting exotic places, making friends that lasted a lifetime, and the loneliness of long periods away from home.

Jack cracked a sweat off the Waikiki Natatorium and, by the time he reached the waters off the Hawaiian Village Hotel a half hour later, the salt that was steadily dripping from his hair stung his eyes. Tired and not excited about the return voyage, he gulped the bottle of water he had brought along and surveyed Honolulu's skyscrapers. From his vantage point two miles out, he imagined the lawyers inside those office buildings who were, at that moment, reviewing documents, preparing for depositions, talking with clients about bills, arguing with each other, and day-dreaming about all the other places they would rather be. He was glad he was in one of those other places.

As he turned his canoe around to begin the voyage home, he heard the roar of silver airliners emerging from the bright blue sky to begin their final approach to Honolulu International Airport. There was no way he could know that one of those air-liners carried a passenger whose fate would soon alter the idyllic life he and Katherine had enjoyed since moving to Oahu.

Forty minutes later, Jack looked up at the left side of the Surf Hotel and then sighted down it to the jetty below, barely visible now because the wind had increased and larger swells washed over the end of the jetty. From his perch on the canoe, Jack looked to his right but did not see the windsock. He sat there for a moment, seaward of the reef, and scanned the surface of the water. He caught a glimpse of the orange windsock as his canoe rose on top of a swell, but it quickly disappeared when the canoe slid down the wave. These quick bearings were sufficient to let Jack position his canoe for the run through the break in the reef. He waited and watched the pattern of the waves behind him, ascertaining when they would reach their peaks and where they would break. His strategy was to pass through the reef behind one breaking wave and in front of another so that he cleared the reef's channel before the wave behind him broke, always mindful that his one-man canoe would not stand up to a pounding on the reef.

As one building wave passed under him and surged toward the reef, he began to paddle slowly. He waited until that wave reached the reef and was about to break, then jabbed his paddle into the water rapidly and repeatedly. He looked behind and saw the next wave building thirty feet astern of his canoe. Jack dug his paddle deeper and turned the boat to the right to keep it headed straight through the channel. After ten hard strokes, he put some distance between himself and the wave behind him, cleared the reef, and surged onto the beach. He had once again completed a successful voyage.

Jack carried his canoe back to its storage rack outside the locker room, showered and dressed, and then walked to the Club's dining room for his second breakfast of the day.

"How was your workout?" Noa asked.

"Pretty good," Jack responded. "I'm getting the hang of it, and I feel stronger in the right places. You know, I'm forty-five, Noa, and it's not as if I haven't put some miles on this body."

"I know what you mean."

Jack opted for his usual breakfast of guava juice, mango with lime, whole wheat toast, and Kona coffee prepared in a French Press. As he shared this exotic coffee with Noa, Jack asked, "Do many members of the Club order Kona coffee here in the dining room?"

"A fair number do. You'd be surprised. It's expensive, but people seem to be willing to pay for it."

Jack nodded, a half smile crossing his lips. "That's great, Noa. Music to my ears."

"I'll bet," Noa replied. "You've got a whole plantation full of Kona coffee over on the Big Island. I know you don't worry about the price — the more it costs, the more you make!"

"Spoken like a veteran Club Manager. By the way, I see from the menu that the coffee you're serving was made from beans grown on my place. Unassailable evidence of your discriminating taste!"

"Jack, you're the best example I know of the old adage that these islands choose you; you don't choose them. When did you give in and decide to move to Hawaii?" Noa asked.

"The first time I saw Diamond Head; it just took me a while to get here," Jack said. "I'm a Pacific guy, Noa. I was meant to live here. Katherine feels the same way. This is the place for us."

"So what's on your mind, Noa? You said you wanted to talk."

"I did. I've got a great opportunity for you. You'll be in my debt forever."

"I already am; you're serving my coffee at Hawaii's most famous club."

"No, I'm not kidding, Jack. Hollywood has come to Honolulu. You may have seen it in the Advertiser. They're filming a big flick out here starring Hypatia Adams, the most elegant actress since Grace Kelly, and the producer is that movie mogul Derek Reynolds. He came out from Los Angeles for a few days, and his production company is honoring him with a party here at the Club tonight. They called this morning and asked me to invite some interesting locals to the party, and I immediately thought of you and Katherine."

"Really?"

"Yes, and you should come. Besides, how many other Monday night parties do you know of?"

"All right. We'll be there. Aloha attire?"

"Yes, we want them to feel the real Hawaii."

"Who are the other 'locals' you've invited?"

"Oh, some you know and some you probably don't know. Arthur Fairbanks, the author, is coming. You know Arthur. I thought we needed a British component. After all, the Brits were here in Hawaii for a while, and our state flag does incorporate the Union Jack."

"Sort of a gesture to Captain Cook," Jack observed.

"Exactly."

"Well, I do know Arthur. He lives at The Royal and he's quite a character. He's eccentric, but one hell of a writer and a good guy to boot. Arthur's either the Somerset Maugham or the Graham Greene of his generation, I'm not sure which. I guess it depends on what he's writing about on any given day. I'll tell you this, Noa. I think he's got an MI-6 background, but he's been mum about it with me so far. Who else is coming?"

"Sidney and George Lane. Do you know them?" Noa asked.

"I met them at the Grant's but I really don't know them well. Anybody else I should know about?"

"Well, I've invited some Navy guys from Pearl Harbor. Maybe you'll run into an old shipmate."

"I doubt it, but I'll look forward to meeting them."

"They're bringing a political guy with them," Noa added, "an Assistant Secretary of the Navy who's in town to meet with the Pacific Fleet commander."

"Okay. We'll look forward to it, Noa. Thanks for thinking of us."

"You're welcome, Jack. By the way, I'll bet Katherine will look better than the movie stars here tonight."

"You can count on that."

CHAPTER TWO

Jack left the Club and headed for Kapahulu Avenue and downtown Honolulu. He was on his way to the Bishop Museum, Hawaii's best collection of Hawaiian artifacts and books about the islands, to do some research on coffee bean production along the Kona coast. As he wound through Honolulu's streets to H-1, which was nearly bumper to bumper as always, Jack reflected on his decision to move to Hawaii. While the seed had probably been planted twenty years ago during his days as a Naval Officer, that experience was not, as lawyers like to point out, the "proximate cause" of his decision to move five thousand miles from the east coast to the middle of the Pacific Ocean. He was an accomplished lawyer, had tried criminal and civil cases, argued important appeals, and enjoyed the law for many years. He probably would have stayed with it if he hadn't taken the six-month sabbatical that every partner took after fifteen years at the firm — and if he hadn't spent it in Hawaii, where he and Katherine had also gone on their honeymoon.

The sabbatical gave Jack time to realize that he wanted to do other things with his life than just practice law. It had begun to gnaw at him several years earlier, and the intensity of the idea grew as the years flew by. Once he conceded that he was not going to live forever, he realized that if he didn't make the break now, he never would.

Approaching the exit from H-1 to the Bishop Museum, Jack recalled the anguish he had experienced before telling the managing partner of his law firm, an austere man who could be difficult. Paul Caldwell Brand, known to the firm as PCB, was a tall, thin man in his early sixties whose wire-rimmed glasses and thick gray hair framed a dark stare fueled by a quick temper. He had survived the cyclical ups and downs of a corporate practice to rise to the top of the firm. But, privately, he knew how fortunate he had been, and this knowledge tempered his occasionally dyspeptic behavior toward those in his charge.

Jack liked him. Paul appealed to his sense of discipline, and imposing discipline on lawyers is like herding cats. Nevertheless, when Jack went to see Paul to tell him that he had decided to resign from the firm, move to Hawaii and grow coffee beans, he expected a tirade followed by the recommendation of a good psychiatrist. Instead, after Jack told PCB of his decision, there was a long silence and an equally poignant exhalation of cigar smoke. Paul looked at him and gently placed his omnipresent cigar on the crystal ashtray at the front of his desk.

"Jack, you're a damn good lawyer," Paul said. "Hell, for the past fifteen years, you've tried the biggest cases this firm has been involved in. On top of that, everybody here likes you. So I'm goddamned sorry to see you leave. But I understand that everyone has their own destiny in life. Everyone has to play the cards that life deals them. You know the hand I was dealt. I played it the best way I knew how and I've been lucky in some ways. In other ways, I haven't been so lucky."

Jack was surprised at Paul's candor but not at the substance of what he had said. PCB had been part of the group that had moved the firm from the traditional practice of law to the modern business world. He had been the point of friction between the old-line lawyers and the new-age, business lawyers, and the former knew that he favored the latter. Now PCB was left with the product of his management – more money and less peace than he had ever had in his life.

"You've obviously persuaded your beautiful and talented wife to leave her law firm as well. And you made a mint on that case you tried a couple years ago. So, why not? But do me a favor. Every once in a while, let me know how you're doing. And Jack, if you change your mind, there will always be a place here for you. Just give me a call."

"Thanks, Paul. I will."

"I'll have the accounting department calculate your share of the partnership, and it will be paid out to you within the month. Now, tell me about that coffee plantation you'll be putting all this money in, Jack."

"It's a small farm on a hill on the Kona Coast of the Big Island of Hawaii. A friend of mine out there showed it to me during my sabbatical. It's got fertile volcanic soil and enough coffee trees to make money, but it's been badly managed over the last few years by some dotcommers who had more money than sense. I'm sure I can turn it into a profitable operation, and Katherine plans to test the fashion waters of the Pacific. She's a dress designer at heart and wants to try her hand at her own dress shop in Honolulu."

"Sounds idyllic, Jack. Send me some beans from your plantation, will you? Kona coffee is hard as hell to find here on the east coast. Almost as hard as these Cubanos are," Paul said, as he opened his humidor and pulled out a fistful of Havana Montecristo Number Six cigars.

"A British client of the firm who knows of my penchant for Cuban cigars dropped these off yesterday. Take a few. They'll be hard to come by where you're going."

"Thank you, Paul. Goodbye."

"Goodbye, Jack, and please give my regards to Katherine. I'm sure her dress designs will be a huge success out there if they even remotely resemble the ones she wears around this town."

"I will." Jack got up from the leather chair, shook Paul's hand, and walked out of the professional life he had known for fifteen years.

Jack snapped out of his reverie just as he reached the entrance to the Bishop Museum. While walking toward the dark red-stoned structure that reminded him of an old university library, he called Katherine on his cell phone to tell her about the cast party that evening at the Club. Then he waded into books about soil conditions, rainfall, sunlight and all the other conditions that affect the growing of coffee beans on the Kona Coast of Hawaii.

At the same time, the Reader was arriving at a field near the Windward Shore town of Kailua. Armed with a sharp knife, shears and a copy of the photograph from the Bishop Museum book, the Reader pulled off the road onto the field and began searching for a particular leaf. Not finding it after ten minutes, the Reader lit a cigarette and surveyed the perimeter of the field. Noticing a clump of brush not evident initially, the Reader walked toward it and discovered the object of the search. Kneeling down and leaning into the bush, the Reader cut several branches of the bush and folded other branches over them to cover the marks. The Reader then walked briskly back to the car, placed the branches in the trunk, grabbed a wet rag to soak up the dangerous fluid that had leaked from the broken branches, and drove away hurriedly. There was not much time to prepare for this evening's party.

CHAPTER THREE

The Royal Hawaiian Hotel, known as the Pink Palace, has always been one of the great hotels of the Pacific. It was built on property that had once been the home of Hawaii's royalty, and its beach was once the playground of the islands' kings and queens. Since the day it opened in 1927, the Royal has reigned over Waikiki Beach.

When Jack and Katherine decided to move to Hawaii, they faced a dilemma. Their coffee farm was on the Big Island of Hawaii, but Katherine's dress business would flourish only if she had access to an urbane and cosmopolitan market. Since they both loved Honolulu and had a circle of friends there, they decided to live in both places.

Katherine would rent space in one of the elegant Waikiki hotels where she could display her designs to tourists and island-ers. Jack would visit their coffee plantation during the week, leaving daily management to Keoni Campbell, an experienced coffee farm manager who lived on the Big Island. And, since the farm came with a traditional Hawaiian plantation house overlooking the Pacific, they would make that their second home, spending weekends and holidays there.

Intrigued by the idea of living on Waikiki Beach, Jack and Katherine went to see the Royal Hawaiian's manager, Peter Dillingham, whom they knew from previous stays at the hotel, and asked if they could rent a suite for a year.

Thinking it might be good for the Royal's atmosphere to have a small cadre of interesting full-time residents, he offered them the choice of a suite on the fifth floor that had a very nice view of Waikiki Beach or a suite in the tower just above the fifth floor that the elevators did not serve but which had a panoramic view of the Pacific. They chose the tower.

Jack made the trip back to the Royal in record time, weaving through the Waikiki traffic that begins to build at four o'clock each day, and dropped his Jeep off at the hotel's entrance. He bounded up the steps to the open air lobby and walked briskly to elevators flanked by old maps depicting the Hawaiian Islands when Captain Cook discovered them in 1778 and named them the Sandwich Islands after one of his patrons. He took the elevator to the fifth floor and walked down a short corridor and up a half flight of stairs to their tower suite. Its location and height afforded Jack and Katherine a wide-angle lens' view of the Pacific from Diamond Head on the left edge to Waikiki Beach in the foreground to Barbers Point on the right edge of the frame, eighteen miles west of the Royal.

"Hellooo!" Jack called as he opened the door to their suite.

"Hellooo!" Katherine responded from the direction of their bedroom.

Hugo, their Maine Coon cat, barely stirred from his perch on top of the chintz-covered chair in the living room and didn't shift his gaze from Waikiki Beach.

"How was your day, Hugo?" Jack inquired as he scratched the cat's head.

Hugo, a dark brown cat with swirls of caramel mixed in on his sides, a snow white chest and stomach, and white paws with a small black spot on his right rear leg, responded by slowly standing up and stretching in a yoga-like movement, first forward and then back. As soon as Jack stopped scratching him, Hugo returned to his strategic post, master of all he surveyed.

"You know," Jack said as he walked into the bedroom, "Hugo has a good deal."

"Well, of course he does. He deserves it; he expects it. This is his place. We're just guests. In fact, as Hugo sees it, he owns this hotel and just lets the tourists stay here and use the beach. When are you going to realize who's in charge?" Katherine said as she finished dressing for the evening.

"Blonde One, you look great," Jack exclaimed as he kissed his green-eyed wife and hugged her in the long silent embrace that was ritual between them.

"So, who's coming to this cast party?" she asked as Jack walked toward the shower.

"Well, first of all, the producer, the director, and the stars will be there — Derek Reynolds, Mark Sandish, Hypatia Adams, and whoever else is in the movie."

"Anybody else?"

"Some locals like us and some Navy people from Pearl Harbor. I think they're bringing some political guy from Washington with them. Arthur Fairbanks will be there."

"Great. If all else fails, I can share a few laughs with Arthur," Katherine said. "Are Gordon and Georgia coming?"

"I hope so, because in my experience, these Hollywood types don't socialize well with outsiders. They gather in one corner of the room and talk to each other."

"Really?" Katherine said. "Then why are we going when we could have a perfectly nice evening at home?"

"Because Noa is the host and he wants us there."

When Jack emerged from the bathroom, Katherine handed him one of his brightly colored silk shirts with a Hawaiian pattern. This one had subtle green and yellow bamboo stalks set against a navy blue background – one of his favorites.

"Do you think this will get Hollywood's attention, Katherine?" Jack smiled.

"Absolutely, my dear."

Jack put on his white cotton trousers and tucked the shirt in, tightening his belt one notch tighter than the last time he had worn it.

"This paddling and running have really gotten me in great shape. I think I've lost another inch off my waist."

"Don't lose too much, Jack," Katherine said with a smile. "I like your body just as it is."

Jack looked in the mirror, brushing his hair and then straightening his shirt, and saw Katherine walking toward him, her image reflected in the full length mirror on the back of the closet door. She was wearing a black silk dress, oriental in its cut with thin straps over the shoulders and a modest slit on one side. Against the black background were splashed large pink Hibiscus and red Poinciana flowers in a colorful tropical pattern that suggested the lush beauty of Hawaii's gardens and hillsides. Her blonde hair was up in a simple twist.

They drove to the Diamond Head in Katherine's white 1968 Mercedes convertible. As they approached the Club, there was a small crowd on the street, hoping to catch a glimpse of the stars. Noa had discreetly let the press know there would be a cast party at the Club, and word had gotten out that celebrity sightings could be had at the Diamond Head.

Out on the beach, a Native Hawaiian band played traditional Hawaiian songs with ukuleles and slack key guitars while a beautiful young girl in a grass skirt performed the hula. All the trappings of a luau were set up in the dining room. The tables offered Kalua Pig, Chicken Long Rice, Lomi Lomi Salmon, Ahi Poke, Laulau and an array of Pacific fish that included the dolphin mahimahi, yellowfin tuna, known in Hawaii as ahi, wahoo, known in Hawaii as ono, opakapaka, a Pacific pink snapper, ehu, a Pacific red snapper, and onaga, a Pacific crimson snapper. There were plates piled high with freshly sliced mangoes, papayas, yams and tomatoes and, next to them, bowls filled with poi, brown rice and white rice.

As Jack and Katherine walked toward the lounge, Noa Watson greeted them warmly.

"Mrs. Sullivan, you look beautiful and, as always, your dress will be the talk of the party. Thank you so much for coming. Jack, you're a lucky man."

"Thank you, Noa," Katherine said.

"I know," Jack said, as a huge hand suddenly clamped on his back.

"Sullivan," the familiar voice of Gordon Grant boomed, "I vanquished McNeil today at the Oahu Country Club. He actually challenged me to 18 holes of golf at my club. You must tend to him. He's desperately in need of one of your Wiki Wiki's. And while you're taking care of Dave, I will tend to your beautiful wife.

"How are you, my dear?" Gordon asked Katherine.

"Wonderful, Gordon, and how are you faring since our last game of Five Up? I heard that you were in a state of depression for several days."

"Ah, I should have known that my charity would go unappreciated."

"Oh, I see," Katherine said. Would you like to play a game here at the Club tonight?"

"I wish I could, Katherine, but duty calls. In my capacity as the President of this establishment, I have grave responsibilities. But may I say that you look ravishing. When Georgia sees that dress, I know she'll want one just like it, and my assets will again decline significantly."

"Think of the dresses your wife wears as assets, Gordon, and, by the way, where is Georgia?"

"She's out by the seawall talking to the star of the movie, Hypatia Adams. You must meet her. She's very nice, not at all a

Hollywood type. And believe me, I know. When I was at USC, I dated them all."

Jack had spotted Dave McNeil a few feet away at the bar, smoking a very fine cigar. Dave was an extraordinary man, fifty years old and in superb physical condition. His crew cut black hair was flecked with gray, his muscles toned by hours of paddling and coaching the Club's women's paddling team. A Midwesterner by birth, he had stayed in the islands after serving in the Marine Corps at Kaneohe Bay and joined the Honolulu Police Department. His wife Nicole was a member of one of the prominent missionary families who had brought both Christianity and capitalism to Hawaii in the middle of the nineteenth century.

Jack put his hand on Dave's back and said, quietly, "I heard you played golf with Grant today."

His head hung low, a Panama hat tilted back on his head, Dave slowly turned away from the bar, recognizing Jack's voice, and said, "Thank you, friend, for charitably characterizing my performance today as playing the game of golf."

"Did he do it to you again?" Jack asked.

"He did. I don't know why I play golf with him. He's not only good at it, he practices psychological warfare on me. When I hit a bad shot, which happens frequently, he doesn't just ignore it out of pity for me. He makes a point of telling me how sad it is that I'm such a terrible golfer. When I stepped up to the first tee, he asked me if I was nervous playing with him. After the ninth hole, he asked me if I could remember the last time I had played so badly. After the round, he suggested that I consider giving up the game."

"I know why you continue to play with him," Jack said. "For the same reason we all do. He's so goddamned much fun to be with. I laugh like hell when I play golf with him. And I tell him every time he hits a bad shot. It infuriates him and incites him to be even more competitive, if that's possible."

"I'll have to give that a try," Dave said.

"How's life treating you otherwise?" Jack asked.

"Excellent. The ladies are paddling better than ever. My own paddling is better than last year. And crime seems to be following the economy down. So life is good. I've got plenty of time for paddling and for my kids. Unfortunately, I've also got time for golf."

"Where's your lovely wife?"

"Nicole couldn't make it. The kids have a soccer banquet tonight, and she's got chaperone duty."

"Well, tell her we said hi. I hope we see you guys soon."

"I hope so too."

CHAPTER FOUR

Jack could see why Noa Watson thought Hypatia Adams was the classiest actress since Grace Kelly. Her presence radiated a vulnerability and magnetism that attracted everyone at the party.

Hypatia was laughing with Georgia Grant when Gordon brought Jack and Katherine over to meet her.

"Hello Diva," Katherine called to Georgia.

Hypatia saw Katherine's dress and exclaimed, "I love your dress. It's just perfect for the islands. May I ask where you got it?"

Georgia tossed her long mane of brown hair, looked at Hypatia, and pronounced in a serious tone, "Hypatia, you simply must get together with Katherine. She designed this dress and, frankly, all the best dresses at this party, including, of course, mine.

"Hello darlings, how are you?" Georgia said, leaning forward to kiss Jack and then Katherine.

"Hypatia, I want you to meet my best friends in all the world, Katherine Sullivan, fashion designer to the most chic women in Honolulu, and Jack Sullivan, lawyer, coffee magnate, and all around good guy."

"It's so nice to meet both of you. Jack, I love your shirt almost as much as Katherine's dress."

"Thank you, Hypatia," Jack replied, surprised that a movie star would notice how he was dressed.

Hypatia turned to Katherine. "Do you have a dress shop here in Honolulu?"

"Yes, I do. It's called Hibiscus and it's in the Halekulani Hotel."

"Could I come over tomorrow?" Hypatia asked. "The screenwriters are revising some scenes, so we have the day off. It's our first free moment since we arrived here, and I'd love to see your designs."

As the women expanded their talk of dresses and high fashion, Jack noticed Arthur Fairbanks, the British novelist and his neighbor at the Royal Hawaiian, standing at the bar, ordering his usual whiskey. Arthur was a distinguished-looking man of medium height with only a wisp of light brown hair left on his head and a sandy mustache that gave the sixty-six year old Brit a dash of flair. He wore his social uniform: a blue, double-breasted blazer with his family's crest on its buttons, gray trousers, a blue-striped shirt with spread collar, and a colorful ascot. That was as close as Arthur ever came to wearing Aloha attire.

Jack approached the bar. "Hello, Arthur, how are you?" he asked.

"Jack, old boy, good to see you, an Atlantic creature like myself, swimming among the denizens of the Pacific. I'm in cracking form. Thank you for inquiring."

As Jack smiled, Arthur continued, "Of course, I hail from the more civilized side of that pond, wouldn't you agree, Jack? But that's why we get along so smashingly. We share an Atlantic heritage."

"You know, Arthur, you're right. That is why we get along so well. Atlantic pasts with a Pacific future."

"Well said, my boy. God Save The Queen!" Arthur exclaimed, lifting his glass of whiskey.

"Now, what else? What's new? Who do you know here? Give me the names."

"Well, I just met the star, Hypatia Adams, and, of course, I know the Grant's and Dave McNeil. I've met Sidney and George Lane but I can't say that I know them."

"Then you're in for an interesting evening. The Lane's go back a long way with the producer of this movie, and it's not a very chipper tale."

"Why? What's their problem?" Jack asked.

"It traces back to their time in California," Arthur explained, "when Sidney thought she'd be the next great movie star and George was counting on that too."

"What happened – not enough talent?"

"Oddly enough," Arthur said, "she had talent. Not nearly as much as she and George thought, but she was a rather good actress with a good singing voice, an unusual combination."

"And?" Jack asked.

"She was never able to make the leap from good movies to great movies. And ol' George really went round the bend, getting more and more frustrated as his financial expectations went unfulfilled. They became prickly toward others in the business, particularly the producers and directors who had, in their view, let them down."

"I suppose that didn't make them very popular on the Hollywood social scene," Jack observed.

"No, it bloody well did not."

"Did she ever get a break and take a shot at the big one?"

"Yes, she did," Arthur said, "and it was tragic. She nearly won the leading role in an epic film. In fact, her agent called and told her that she'd been selected. But, at the last minute, the producer changed his mind and selected a 'close friend' of the director for the lead role."

"That must have been tough on Sidney," Jack said.

"Yes it was, and equally so for George. She gave up after that. As you Yanks say, she threw in the towel, hung it up. And they moved to Hawaii, where George continued to work in banking, which had been his business in Los Angeles."

"What happened to the movie?" Jack asked.

"It was an utter flop, one of those movies that Hollywood spends the Queen's ransom on, hypes with an enormous marketing budget, and then watches fail in the most miserable fashion."

"I suppose that gave the Lane's a modicum of satisfaction."

"On the contrary, it made them even angrier. The way they saw it, if Sidney had been given the lead role, the movie would have been a spectacular success. And they may have been right. There was enormous criticism in the Hollywood press about the complete lack of chemistry between the lead actor and actress."

"How do you know all this, Arthur?"

"Because I consulted on the screenplay and I knew all the players. In fact, here comes one right now."

Jack looked toward the lobby of the Diamond Head and saw Noa greeting a man with quite a bit of attention and deference.

"Who is that, Arthur?"

"That is Derek Reynolds, the producer."

"The one who bumped Sidney and gave the lead to the director's paramour?"

"Indeed."

"Then this ought to be quite an interesting evening," Jack said, watching people flock to greet Derek.

"Frankly, I can't believe that Sidney and George would want to be in the same room with Derek, much less guests at a party honoring the cast of his latest movie," Arthur said.

"Why would they do that to themselves?"

"I don't know, Jack, but I must say hello to Derek. For all of his warts, he is one of Hollywood's most successful producers, and I've worked with him on several projects. Pop over in a bit with Katherine, and I shall make the proper introductions. Oh, by the way, Jack," Arthur added, "there's something you should know before you meet Derek."

"What's that?"

"He's been involved with Hypatia for about a year now, but I hear things aren't going well."

"What do you mean?"

"There have been some rumors about the police being called to her house in the middle of the night."

"Not good." Jack said.

"I just mention it because I know you and Katherine, and I have no doubt that by the end of this little soiree, you will have invited Derek and Hypatia to one of those dinner parties you two are so well known for. And if what I hear is true, they may not be a couple much longer."

"How do they work together?" Jack asked.

"They don't. Derek leaves the day-to-day production matters to his underlings. He selects the director and gives him nearly complete discretion."

"So why is he here tonight?"

"He flew to Hawaii last weekend and tried to have a talk with Hypatia about their future or, should I say, the lack of it. He saw her last weekend over on the Big Island, and is scheduled to fly back to Los Angeles tomorrow."

"How'd it turn out?"

"I hear not well. He reacted badly when she said she wanted to end their relationship. If her sister hadn't been with her, I think there might have been trouble. He's a volatile man."

"Thanks for the warning, Arthur. I think we'll wait until that matter gets resolved before issuing any invitations."

Jack glanced out toward the seawall and saw that Katherine, Georgia, and Hypatia were still engaged in animated conversation, so he turned back toward the bar and saw Dave lighting his second cigar of the evening. Noa waved to him and beckoned him toward the lobby, where he was standing with three men wearing Aloha shirts. By their bearing, Jack knew immediately that they must be the Pearl Harbor contingent.

"Jack, I want you to meet Admiral Andrew Simmons, Commander of the Pacific Fleet," Noa said, adding, "I've told him all about you."

"Very nice to meet you, sir," Jack responded, reverting instinctively to his former status as a Navy Lieutenant.

"Jack, it's great to meet you. Please call me Andy."

"It's a deal, as long as you don't call me Lieutenant," Jack replied with a smile.

"Let's shake on it," the Admiral rejoined, extending a well-tanned arm and strong hand.

"Jack, I want you to meet some colleagues of mine. This is Commander Tom Butler, skipper of the *USS Halsey*, the finest Destroyer in the Pacific Fleet. You can call him Tom, and Tom, you can call him Jack," the Admiral said with a loud laugh.

"I'm pleased to meet you, sir," the Commander said to Jack.

"Old habits die hard," the Admiral observed as he looked around for the third member of their party, who was talking to Noa.

"Jack, let me introduce you to the political component of our delegation, Richard Stanley, the best Assistant Secretary of the Navy to visit Hawaii in a long time."

"Nice to meet you, Jack. Noa gave us a brief on who we'd meet tonight, and you and I have a lot in common."

"It's good to meet you, Richard," Jack replied.

"Please, I go by Rich."

"I'll look forward to talking with you, Rich."

"Let me take these gentlemen to the bar for some drinks, Jack, and then join us there," Noa said, obviously pleased that three of the Navy's finest representatives in Hawaii had accepted his invitation.

Just as Jack decided it was time to drag Katherine away from Hypatia and visit with some of their friends, he ran smack into Sidney and George Lane who were walking toward him from the bar, drinks in hand.

"Hello, Sidney. Hello, George," Jack said as they met.

"Hello, Jack," said George. Sidney was looking elsewhere, searching the room, when her husband touched her arm and reminded her that Jack had just said hello.

"I'm sorry, Jack. But I was looking for that lowlife Reynolds. If I see him, I just may let him know what a Diamond Head Mai Tai looks like, all over his face."

"Sidney, come on," George said. "I knew we shouldn't have come here tonight. I'm sorry, Jack, but I'm afraid some people here stir very unpleasant memories for Sidney and, frankly, for me."

"Well, George, life can do that."

"Yes, it can," Sidney said.

It was obvious that the Mai Tai in Sidney's hand was not her first of the evening.

"George," Sidney said in a firm voice, "you may not want to join me, but I'm going over and say hello to the biggest prick Hollywood ever created, and I hope I can restrain myself."

With that, Sidney and George proceeded, Mai Tai's in hand, toward Derek Reynolds. Jack averted his eyes, waiting for the crash, but it didn't come. Instead, it appeared that the three of them were engaged in civil conversation.

Jack decided it was time to retrieve Katherine and headed for the seawall. A young woman had joined the group, a younger version of Hypatia, not quite as tall, but with the same shade of blonde hair and similarly elegant features. She was talking with Katherine, while Hypatia listened to Georgia describe the high quality of the local theater on Oahu. As Jack approached, Katherine turned toward him and said, "Jack, this is Hypatia's sister Jennifer. She flew in from Los Angeles last week to spend the weekend and has decided to stay for a while."

"Very nice to meet you, Jennifer. How are you enjoying Hawaii?"

"Fine, for the most part. Although, as I was just telling your wife, the company my sister has been keeping leaves a bit to be desired."

"Well, there are plenty of nice people on Oahu, and many of them will be here tonight," Jack said.

"It's not the Oahu people I'm referring to, Jack. It's the Hollywood people and one in particular. Katherine will tell you all about him."

"Okay," Jack said, wishing he weren't there, but quickly adding, "Katherine, how would you like to meet the Commander of the Pacific Fleet?"

"I'd love to." Katherine was an inveterate reader of national security thrillers.

"Would you excuse us, Jennifer?" Jack asked.

"Absolutely, I've got to watch out for my sister anyway, in case that jerk Reynolds comes this way."

"Jennifer, please don't refer to Derek in that tone," Hypatia said.

"He's a creep, Hypatia, and if he comes near us, he'll regret it."

With that, Hypatia excused herself and moved Jennifer down the seawall toward the beach, where no one was standing.

"Georgia, we're going over to meet the Admiral. Want to join us?"

"No thanks, Jack, I think I'll see if Gordon needs any help managing this party."

As Jack and Katherine walked toward the bar where Admiral Simmons was entertaining some guests, Jack asked what Jennifer had said about Derek Reynolds.

"It seems that Derek is a really erratic guy, prone to fits of anger, very possessive of Hypatia, very jealous, and way too high strung. He fancies himself a ladies man and even flaunts it, if you can imagine that."

"Why is Jennifer so exercised about him tonight?" Jack asked.

"Because he's been pushing Hypatia around and she wants to end their relationship, but he won't let her. He won't go away. And when they met last weekend on the Big Island, things apparently got worse."

"What happened?"

"It's very strange. Jennifer flew in from Los Angeles to spend the weekend with Hypatia on the Big Island to get some sun and relax on the beach. They were staying at The Poinciana, just two sisters having a girls' weekend, when Derek showed up out of nowhere and told Jennifer to leave."

"I'll bet that didn't sit well with Jennifer."

"I don't think Hypatia was too thrilled with it either."

Jack and Katherine had reached the bar. Admiral Simmons was holding court, and it was obvious why the Navy had chosen him to lead the Pacific Fleet. He dominated the conversation, even to the exclusion of the Assistant Secretary, who was barely staying awake, having just arrived in Hawaii from Washington after thirteen hours of airports, airplanes, cars and a five-hour time difference. As he approached the Admiral, Jack noticed that Commander Butler was walking toward Hypatia and Jennifer, who were still standing at the seawall.

"Admiral, I want you to meet my wife, Katherine."

"It's a pleasure, Katherine, and I hope you'll call me Andy."

"I would be delighted, Andy," Katherine said as she extended her hand to shake his.

"I must warn you, Andy, that Katherine reads all the national security and naval thrillers and she is well-versed in foreign intrigue," Jack said.

"Wonderful," the Admiral replied. "Katherine, what do you think of this Middle East situation?"

As Katherine engaged the Admiral in a lively discussion, Jack saw that the Assistant Secretary was fading fast.

"Rich, can I give you some advice about adjusting to the time zone here in Hawaii?"

"Please!"

"I know that your body time is closing in on two o'clock in the morning. I also know that you've now been up for about twenty-one hours if you took the early morning flight from Washington through Los Angeles."

"You're right. I'm dead on my ass."

"I know the feeling, and I have a suggestion. Some say the cure is worse than the ailment, but it's worked for me."

"Anything. What is it?"

"You're not going to like this, but you've got to stay awake for another two and a half hours, until eleven o'clock. Then, you'll sleep eight hours and wake up on Hawaii time, more or less, tomorrow morning."

"Great. How do I do that?"

"Keep talking. Keep standing. And don't think about it. You've only got a little while to go, but if you give up now and go back to your hotel, it will take you two days to get on Hawaii time."

"I'll do it. I don't want to make this any harder than it has to be."

"Good. So what do we have in common that Noa told you about?"

"Jack, I'm a recovering lawyer," Richard pronounced in a somber tone.

Jack howled upon hearing the phrase that had recently gained popularity in legal circles, describing lawyers who had left the private practice of law for other endeavors.

"How do you feel?" Jack asked.

"You know, Jack, I feel good so far. I haven't missed it yet. Do you?"

"Oh, every once in a while, I get the urge to try a case, but it usually passes. Not always, though, I have to admit."

"I know what you mean. You can't get it completely out of your system, even after you leave it," Rich said.

"That's true. Say Rich, where did Commander Butler go? I want to hear about that new Destroyer he commands."

"Jack, it's the damnedest thing. We're standing here sipping these Mai Tai's, when he turns to me and says he knows Hypatia Adams. He dated her in California before she became a star."

"Did he know she'd be here tonight?"

"No, his ship just arrived in Pearl this weekend for antisubmarine warfare exercises, and this is the first time he's been off the ship. Admiral Simmons called him this afternoon and ordered him to join us tonight, to get him away from the ship for some R&R."

"What a pleasant surprise for Tom."

"Yes. He got very excited when he saw her. I don't think they've talked since she hit the big time.

"Jack, would you excuse me for a moment. There's a local politico here, and the Secretary of the Navy asked me to be sure to say hello to him. I just spotted him across the room."

"Of course," Jack said. "But don't violate Rule One and go to sleep before eleven o'clock."

"I won't and thanks for the advice. I hope we can get together while I'm here in Honolulu."

"Absolutely. Where are you staying?"

"I'm at the Royal Hawaiian."

"Great! That's where we live. We'll be in touch."

"Thanks, Jack," Rich said as he walked toward the Mayor of Honolulu.

Turning toward Katherine and Admiral Simmons, Jack saw Jennifer Adams out of the corner of his eye, standing next to Derek Reynolds, sipping Mai Tai's with him and appearing for all intents and purposes as his long lost friend. First it was Sidney and George Lane enjoying Hawaii's favorite libation with the producer who had ruined her career and his finances, and now it was Jennifer Adams with the guy who was abusing her sister.

Hollywood people are truly strange, Jack concluded.

CHAPTER FIVE

Katherine had the look that she generally reserved for filet mignon just before she sliced into it. Instead of a steak however, the object of her attention was Admiral Simmons. She wielded her knowledge of international affairs like a steak knife, slicing issues and presenting them to him for consideration, debate and resolution. Simmons was clearly enjoying the moment, not only because Katherine was easy on the eyes, but also because she knew what she was talking about. Jack decided not to interrupt them and instead walked over to Arthur Fairbanks who was talking to one of the cast members.

"Arthur, my good man, you aren't discussing one of your screenplays, are you?"

"How on earth did you know, Jack?"

"I just guessed, although it was a close call between your screenplays and Captain James Cook's impact on Hawaii."

"Indeed. And I am gratified to see that you continue to educate yourself on the Pacific voyages of Britain's greatest explorer. Jack, I would like to present to you Robert Claridge, who starred in 'London Nights', for which I wrote the screenplay nearly ten years ago."

"Robert, it's a pleasure to meet you. I haven't seen 'London Nights', but I've seen some of your other movies and I've enjoyed them very much."

"Thank you, Jack. I was just telling Arthur how much better the screenplay for this movie would be if he had written it. Derek has a bad habit of hiring his friends and his friends' friends to work on his movies, rather than finding the person best for the job."

"You'd think that would catch up with him after a while," Jack said.

"Yes, you would," Robert replied. "But Hollywood is a funny place. You can go a long way just by taking care of your friends and their friends. After a while, you've taken care of so many people that they all start thinking you're brilliant and your movies are magnificent."

"What about the audience?" Jack asked.

"What about them? They read a glowing review written by someone Derek has taken care of. They see an ad in the newspaper prepared by his public relations firm. If they don't like the movie, they think there's something wrong with them, not with the movie."

"Maybe Hollywood isn't as different as I thought," Jack observed.

"Well, it's a bit different," Robert said, "because in this business, we get stuck with bad scripts and have to make some sense out of them."

"Are you having problems with this one?" Jack asked.

"Yes, we are, and many of us are very damn unhappy with the script Derek stuck us with."

"You could quit, couldn't you?"

"Of course we could. But like any other business, you don't want to get a reputation as a quitter or as someone who's hard to work with."

"So you bite the bullet and make a movie you're not exactly thrilled with," Jack said.

"Yes. We all make movies we're not proud of and just hope that nobody in the business or the public is too hard on us. And, I hasten to add, we do need the money. LA mansions are very expensive."

"Well, Arthur, I think it's time I met this infamous producer. Would you do the honors?" Jack asked.

"I would be delighted. Just try to act as if you haven't heard anything about him, if you wouldn't mind. He will sense it immediately if you give him the slightest indication that his reputation has preceded him."

"Don't get your knickers in a twist, Arthur. I'll be on my best behavior."

Arthur took Jack across the room to meet Derek Reynolds who was regaling a comely reporter from the Honolulu Star Advertiser with his plans to shoot more movies in Hawaii and maybe even film a new television series in the Hawaiian Islands. As they approached, Jack heard Derek whisper to the reporter that he'd love to tell her more about his plans for the TV series over breakfast at his hotel the next morning.

Jack was surprised at how ordinary Derek looked. Reynolds was a good seven inches short of six feet. His thinning brown hair reflected the valiant but fruitless efforts of a very skilled plastic surgeon, while his orange-hued face suggested regular visits to the tanning salon. And his developing paunch evidenced a long time since his last visit to the gym. If Jack had passed Derek on the street, he thought, he would barely have noticed him. He looked like any other short, fat, bald guy closing in on sixty and fighting off the grim reaper with little success.

As Arthur introduced him to Derek, however, Jack saw the other side of Derek Reynolds. Derek's eyes quickly narrowed and he looked askance at Jack, sizing him up as a potential adversary. His body tensed as he shook Jack's hand, and he squeezed it hard, obviously trying to make Jack wince. Jack had one thought: this guy is a major league asshole.

Ignoring Jack, Reynolds turned to Arthur.

"So, Fairbanks, what are you doing out here in the middle of nowhere — searching for inspiration?"

"Actually, I do find these islands quite inspiring, Derek, and I assume you do too or you wouldn't be filming your latest movie out here."

"Hardly," Reynolds replied. "Hawaii's economy isn't booming so much that you can't drive a hard bargain. The Japanese aren't coming here in the numbers they used to because their economy is in the tank, and plenty of Americans on the mainland still think it's too far to go for a swim. So I drove a hard bargain and got cheap rates for the scenes I needed to film out here. You name them — carpenters, electricians, plumbers, construction workers, the city, the state, the extras — these people haven't seen a real buck in so long they wouldn't recognize one if somebody showed them a framed picture of George Washington. They're willing to work for rates I couldn't possibly get on the mainland. Now what's your friend Mr. Sullivan doing here in Hawaii?"

"I'm a lawyer and a coffee farmer and, by the way, you can call me Jack."

"I never call anybody by their first name until I decide I want to. You know, Mr. Sullivan, I've burned out a lot of lawyers in my time. I have no respect for them. They're so easy to push around. You ask them to do work for you, hard work. They do it and they even do it well. Then you tell them that you weren't completely satisfied; that you think they didn't have to do everything they did or charge you as much as they did; and you tell them you may not use them the next time; and, if they still argue with you, then you tell them that you ought to sue them for malpractice. After I throw all that at them, you know what they do? They cut their fees. No self- respect. Just another vendor I have to deal with."

With that pronouncement, Derek lifted his Mai Tai and sucked the contents of the glass until it held only ice, a sugar cane swizzle stick, and two chunks of pineapple speared on a soggy paper umbrella toothpick that had fallen into the cocktail while he was drinking it.

"Fairbanks, get me another one of these umbrella drinks. I want to talk to this lawyer," Reynolds said.

"Be careful with those drinks, Derek, they pack a punch that sneaks up on you," Jack warned.

"Mr. Sullivan, I've had three already, and they haven't affected me a bit. In fact, two of them were brought to me on silver platters. One by Sidney Lane, that over-the-hill broad who thinks she's still a star and one by Jennifer Adams, that hottie over there at the seawall. And I haven't fallen down, have I? Trust me, I can handle these umbrella drinks, but dealing with those two broads in one night is enough to make me sick without drinking any liquor."

At that moment, Arthur Fairbanks arrived with Reynolds' fourth Mai Tai of the evening. Reynolds grabbed it from his hand and took a big slug.

"See, Mr. Sullivan. I'm just fine. Don't you worry about me."

"I was just warning Derek about the way Mai Tai's can slip up on you," Jack said to Arthur.

"Oh, quite. Derek, you should be careful."

"Where's Hypatia?" Reynolds said loudly, dismissing Arthur's admonition with a hint of anger in his voice. "She's never around when I want her. It's her goddamned sister's fault. She spends her life telling Hypatia to get rid of me. But it won't happen. Hypatia will never leave me. She can't leave me. She needs me."

Jack and Arthur looked at each other, and Jack decided it was time to find Katherine.

"Derek, I've got to find my wife. It was nice meeting you. Good luck with your movie."

As Arthur Fairbanks started to say goodbye to Reynolds, the producer abruptly turned his back and walked toward the seawall.

"Not likely to win any congeniality awards, is he?" Jack said to Arthur.

"He's a dreadful man, Jack, who doesn't know the meaning of respect. Hypatia simply must get away from him, and I hope Jennifer convinces her to leave him soon."

"I hope so too. He's one of those guys."

"What do you mean?"

"There's a certain kind of man, Arthur, who looks harmless and knows he looks harmless. But he's not. He's the best evidence I know that appearances are deceiving. This sort of guy is frequently bent on doing harm. He's angry and resentful, even when he's been financially and professionally successful. I saw guys like this on juries where they took out their anger on innocent parties. I saw them in corporations where they tried to block the progress of younger guys showing promise. And I've seen them try to control vulnerable women in ways that are manipulative and deceitful. They are just plain bad guys."

"Righto Jack, you've just summed up Derek. I've seen him do all of those things. His kind is dangerous, all the more so because he appears so banal, so innocuous, so ordinary. And, most offensive of all, Jack, he is a complete and utter bore," Arthur concluded with a flourish as he adjusted his ascot.

"Amen," Jack replied.

CHAPTER SIX

As Commander Butler walked toward the seawall, images of his time with Hypatia flashed through his mind — trips to beach towns along the Southern California coast, dinners at quiet places, talks about their lives, hopes and dreams, and reassuring each other that no matter what else happened, they had each other.

"Hypatia," Tom said softly as he reached the Club's seawall. "Tom." They embraced warmly, and then Hypatia turned to Jennifer and said, "Tom, look how my little sister has grown up."

"Hello, Jennifer," Tom said, adding, "Do you remember me?"

"Of course I do. How could I forget you standing at our front door in your white uniform?"

"That seems like a long time ago, especially when I look at you now and remember the last time I saw you. I think you had pigtails then. But one thing hasn't changed."

"What's that?" Jennifer said.

"You're still looking after your big sister. Every time I took Hypatia out, you'd ask me where we were going and what time we'd be home."

"You looked after her too, Tom," Jennifer said. "No one took better care of Hypatia than you did."

Tom blushed, and Hypatia put her arm in his, looked in his dark eyes, and said, "Jennifer's right, you know. No one took care of me like you did."

"I think I'll leave you two alone." Jennifer turned and walked toward the bar.

"So, how are things?" Tom asked.

"Not good," Hypatia said. "This picture is driving me crazy, and I've got a big problem in my social life."

"Tell me about it."

"It's complicated as usual."

"No surprise there," Tom said.

"I never seem to get it right, Tom. I vacillate between good guys like you and bad guys like the one I'm stuck with now."

"Well, you don't have to be stuck with anyone, Hypatia."

"I'm usually pretty good at telling men that it's not going anywhere, and they generally accept it and move on. But this guy won't listen and I'm afraid he never will. I really don't know what to do. That's why Jennifer is so upset."

"Who is it?" Tom asked.

"Derek Reynolds, the producer of this movie."

"I suppose starring in his movie hasn't made things any simpler," Tom said.

"No, it hasn't. I should never have accepted this role, but it's hard to turn down a part in a well-financed movie. You can't do that too many times before they stop calling you."

"So you're stuck with him until this movie is finished. How bad can that be?" Tom asked.

"It's bad, Tom. He's not like you. He's not a gentleman. He has a terrible temper and he threatens me all the time."

"Then you've got to get rid of the son of a bitch now."

"I just don't know how. I really don't. I tried last weekend when he arrived, uninvited and unannounced, at my hotel on the Big Island. He insinuated himself into a weekend that Jennifer and I had planned to talk about girl things. It's as if he knows I'm trying to find a way to break up with him, and he's bound and determined to do everything he can to stop me. He and Jennifer had an awful argument in the hotel's dining room, right in front of everyone. I'm embarrassed to go back. Thank God, there weren't many people there, and nobody recognized me. It didn't make the newspapers or the gossip rags."

"What did he say to you?" Tom asked.

"The usual. I wouldn't be anything if it weren't for him. I owe all my success to him. If I leave him now, he'll ruin my career. He treats me like a possession."

"What a shit!" Tom exclaimed. "That asshole isn't responsible for your talent or your beauty. He just wants to own it."

"You know, Tom, that's exactly what I think." Hypatia's eyes filled with tears.

Tom embraced her, held her close, and whispered in her ear, "I'll help you get out of this. And I'll get you out of it now."

"Oh Tom, I don't want to cause another scene in public. Let me work this out myself."

Suddenly, a loud and obviously intoxicated voice rasped at them.

"What do we have here — a rehearsal session for *From Here to Eternity*?"

It was Reynolds, slurring his words and staggering.

"Derek, this is Tom Butler, an old friend of mine from California."

"Well, Mr. Butler, I'm also an old friend of hers from California. So where do you fit into the picture?"

"Derek, it's Commander Butler," Hypatia said. "Tom is the Commanding Officer of a Destroyer at Pearl Harbor."

"Tora, Tora, Tora, Commander. Let's go, honey, you're going inside now." Reynolds grabbed Hypatia's arm and pulled her away from Tom. "I've had enough of this tropical paradise shit and these stupid shirts and Aloha or whatever they call it."

Tom saw Hypatia wince. He also saw the marks that Reynolds' grip left on her arm.

"Let go of her, asshole," he said.

"What did you say?" Reynolds asked, raising his voice.

"I told you to take your hand off her or I'm going to stick it so far up your ass you'll need an oral surgeon to cut your fingernails."

Reynolds released Hypatia's arm and looked at her with disbelief. "You know this is going to come back on you. I'll ruin you and your sister. You'll end up a 'has been' like that Lane broad and her pathetic husband. Go over and talk to them and see how they like living in the middle of the Pacific on a banker's salary. As for you, Mr. Boy Scout, I wouldn't count on another promotion. I know the President. And he appointed the Secretary of Defense. And I don't think either of them would promote an officer who threatened one of their most generous political contributors."

Reynolds lurched toward the bar where he was immediately surrounded by guests who had not yet met the great man.

"Tom, you shouldn't have done that. He'll get you. He's a powerful man."

"I'm not worried. The guy's an asshole, and everybody knows it. He won't dare go after me. Besides, I'm more concerned about you. And I think I just got you on the road to solving your problem."

"I don't know, Tom. I'm worried. He's a volatile man."

"I can see that," Tom said. "But you had to stand up to him sometime and he gave me the perfect opportunity to help you out. I had to do it."

"I'm actually glad you did," Hypatia said, starting to laugh. Where did you get that line about the oral surgeon?"

"I was inspired," Tom said, as he put his arm around her, and looked out over the seawall to the Pacific.

"We've got to spend more time together. But, for the moment, let's talk about how we first met at the Beach and Tennis Club in San Diego."

"You would remember that one," Hypatia said with a throaty laugh.

"That's because I had to get rid of another guy that time too," Tom said.

"Yes, but he was an old boyfriend I grew up with."

"They're the best kind to get rid of."

"You're right," Hypatia said, with a knowing smile. "But I'm still worried about you. Derek knows lots of politicians because he gives them so much money."

"Don't worry a bit," Tom said. "The Secretary of Defense and I are friends. I served as his Naval Aide when he first worked in the Pentagon as an Under Secretary of Defense in the last Administration. He knows a bad guy when he sees one."

CHAPTER SEVEN

Georgia Grant looked at Katherine Sullivan and exclaimed, "Katherine, look over at the bar! Isn't that someone famous talking to Kulani?"

Katherine glanced at the bar and saw a young man in his mid-to late twenties talking to the Club's bartender.

"I don't think he's famous but I think I've seen his picture somewhere. Maybe he's one of the actors," Katherine said.

"That's it," Georgia exclaimed. "His picture was in *People* magazine not too long ago. He's somebody's boy toy in Hollywood. I think it's Barbara Franklin."

"You're right," Katherine said. "I remember seeing it. I probably still have it at home. But she's pretty old for him. I'll bet she's fifty."

"I'm going to confirm it," Georgia announced as she started toward the bar where the young man was still talking to Kulani.

"Well, hello, I'm Georgia Grant. My husband is President of the Club, and we're your hosts this evening," she said to the young man while also waving to Kulani behind the bar.

"Good evening, Mrs. Grant," he responded with a confident air. "My name is Lance Forbes. I'm a member of the cast and I'm pleased to meet you."

"I'm an actress myself," Georgia said with a smile, "and I'm thrilled that Derek Reynolds is shooting part of his movie here on Oahu."

"Do you know Derek?" Lance asked.

"No. I just met him this evening but I've admired his movies over the years."

"So have I," Lance said. "He's got a real eye for talent. He can spot potential stars before anyone else and he exploits their abilities better and faster than any producer I know. That's why I tried out for a part in this movie."

"You want to be discovered — a commendable, if difficult, goal," Georgia said with a smile that spoke eloquently of her own experience.

"Yes, but with Derek, it can happen. He knows talent and he's not afraid to cast an unknown in one of his movies." Lance spoke in a condescending tone, then turned away and ordered another drink from the bartender.

"Have I seen you in anything else?" Georgia asked.

"No, but you will soon, and in bigger roles."

"Shall I get your autograph now?"

"No. There will be plenty of time for that later."

"Well, I hope this is your moment, Lance," Georgia said graciously. "I'm afraid I have some hostess obligations to fulfill, so I will thank you now for joining us this evening."

"You're quite welcome, Mrs. Grant," Lance said in a slightly dismissive tone.

Georgia returned to Katherine who was talking to another member of the cast.

"Georgia, this is Martha Sutherland. We were just talking about the dresses she wears in her role as a World War II-era socialite here in Honolulu."

"Why then, you must be playing my mother," Georgia said.

"Really," said Martha. "Do you have any photographs of your mother in evening gowns from that period?"

"I certainly do and I'd love to show them to you."

"I'm going to drop by Katherine's shop tomorrow morning with Hypatia," Martha said. "Could we meet there, say at 10:30?"

"Wonderful," Georgia said. "I'll bring my photo album and some Kona coffee. And I'll tell you all about Mother. She was the star of Honolulu's social scene in her day."

"I'm not a bit surprised," Martha said. "I can't wait! I'm going home right now to get the first decent night's sleep since we started shooting. The schedule here has us on the set by seven each morning, and it will be such a luxury to sleep in until eight tomorrow."

As Martha walked away, Katherine turned to Georgia and whispered, "Were we right? Is he Barbara Franklin's boy toy?"

"I'm sure he is, although I didn't ask and he didn't mention her name."

"I'll look through some old *People* magazines I have at home. Maybe he's in there."

"He kept calling me Mrs. Grant."

"Well, my dear, he obviously likes older women," Katherine said. "How old is Barbara Franklin?"

"She's at least 55," said Georgia. "I don't like this 'Mrs. Grant' business. I'm not at that stage, am I?"

"Hardly, Georgia. I'm sure he was more than thrilled to talk to you. What man wouldn't be?"

"Apparently not Mr. Forbes."

"Enough about him. Let's go find Mr. Sullivan and Mr. Grant," Katherine said, taking her arm.

CHAPTER EIGHT

Gordon and Jack were standing at the edge of the Club's dining room, near the Lanai, and Gordon was chewing on the stick of sugar cane that served swizzle duty in his Mai Tai.

Watching Gordon immerse the stick in his drink, Jack asked, "How long do you have to live in Hawaii before these things look and taste less like wood and more like sugar?"

"This, my good man," Gordon responded, lifting the stick clear of his Mai Tai, "is an acquired taste."

Frowning, Jack replied, "As far as I can tell, the only taste that stick has acquired is wood. I don't know why bartenders even bother putting them in Mai Tai's. They don't affect the taste. In fact, they're misleading. They look sweet but they're not."

"You've missed the point entirely," Gordon said. "Mai Tai's are made with different kinds of rum. And where does rum come from? Sugar Cane. So this humble wooden-like stick reminds us of the genesis of the exotic pleasure and sense of peace that Mai Tai's bestow on all who consume them, particularly if they were made by Kulani here at the premier club in the Pacific."

"I see," Jack said. "Personally, I stand with McNeil on this one. I mean if you're going to chew on something while you drink a Mai Tai, it might as well be a good cigar."

"I don't completely disagree with you," Gordon said, "although I hate to see you agree with someone I have so badly vanquished on the golf course. If it got out that you agreed with Dave, it could affect your standing at the Club."

"Where have you two been all night?" Georgia asked as she and Katherine approached the two men.

"Well, we know where the two of you have been," Gordon responded. "Is there any member of the cast you two haven't met tonight?"

"I don't think so. Do you, Katherine?"

"I believe we've covered them all," Katherine said in mock seriousness.

"And not only have we met them, we've had very interesting conversations that will continue tomorrow morning at Katherine's shop over that wonderful Kona coffee Jack brought us from his plantation last week," Georgia said.

"Yes. Hypatia and Jennifer Adams and Martha Sutherland are coming by the shop tomorrow morning to see some of my things and to see pictures of Georgia's mother," Katherine said.

"Well, that's great," Jack said. "Maybe one of your dresses will find its way into this movie."

"You never know," Katherine said.

"By the way, Jack, that last batch of Kona coffee you gave us is superb," Gordon said. "I brew it in my office, and the mere aroma of that stuff infuses my staff with the desire to give me spontaneous status reports over coffee."

"Wonderful! I'm going over to the Big Island in the morning and I'll bring some more back," Jack said.

At that moment, the Hawaiian music stopped, and Noa Watson asked for everyone's attention. Those who were out by the seawall and on the Club's Lanai moved into the dining room.

"Thank you all for joining us this evening here at the Diamond Head Canoe Club," Noa said in his mellifluous Hawaiian tones. "We are so happy to have so many friends from all walks of life on this beautiful island, from our political leaders to our business community to our good friends from the Navy to our artists. We are honored that Hollywood's finest actors, actresses, directors, and producers chose our Club for their cast party, and we wish you the best of luck with this movie and much Aloha."

Everyone applauded, and then Noa announced, "It is my honor to present the man who brought this production to Hawaii, Derek Reynolds. May I ask all of you to raise your glasses in a toast to the good fortune and health of our honored guest."

Reynolds moved haltingly toward Noa in a barely controlled lurch and took the microphone from him.

"I didn't want to make this movie in Hawaii. I'm from California, and we build sets in our studios there that rival any place on earth. And we can generally do it cheaper, too. But my staff came out here, took a look at what you had to offer, and told me I'd be out of my mind not to film most of this movie here on Oahu. So I decided to give it a try."

As Reynolds paused, Jack leaned over to Katherine and whispered, "Quite an eloquent fellow."

"And considerate too," Katherine whispered, "particularly since most of Honolulu's political and business leaders are here."

"But I'm not going to pay for one damn night of hotel rooms that I don't have to, and I'm going to keep this movie on schedule and on budget. It looks to me as if this cast is having a lot more fun out here than they would back in L.A., and that usually means a longer shooting schedule. But not under my rules! As soon as this rewrite is complete, back on the set at seven sharp. That's my message to the cast. I hope the rest of you didn't mind that little bit of motivational oratory."

As Reynolds paused again, Gordon leaned over to Jack and said, "I think old Derek is blasted."

"Either that or he's got a lousy personality," Jack whispered back.

"Or both," Georgia said, loud enough for those around to hear.

"Mr. Watson," Reynolds resumed, "my thanks to you and your Club for hosting our cast party. Send the bill to the director. It'll come out of his share of the profits." He pointed at Mark Sandish.

Tom Butler glanced at Hypatia, who looked mortified, and observed, "This is going downhill fast."

Jennifer, who was standing at the edge of the dining room with her sister and Tom, leaned over to Tom and said, "See what an asshole he is."

By now, everyone had quietly concluded that Derek had had too many Mai Tai's, but he didn't stop.

"Mr. Mayor, we might have the premiere here, if the City throws us a big enough party. And maybe the Admiral will give us one of his ships for the evening." Derek was now slurring his words and having trouble maintaining his balance.

"You can probably get the money out of the bankers here tonight, Mr. Mayor. I'm sure they'd be happy to finance the premiere of one of my movies." Reynolds, now swaying back and forth, was looking directly at George Lane.

Then he turned and looked at Hypatia, Jennifer and Tom. His eyes narrowed and his face was flushed. He started to speak but suddenly stopped with a sharp intake of breath and fell to the floor, his legs folding underneath him.

The crowd gasped as Noa cleared an area around the crumpled figure. Dave McNeil ran over and examined him closely, putting his hand on Derek's wrist to feel his pulse. It was weak.

Dave yelled to Kulani who was behind the bar and told him to call an ambulance. Then, with Noa assisting, Dave began to administer CPR. They were still at it ten minutes later when the ambulance arrived and the emergency medical technicians placed Derek on oxygen and took him out of the Club on a gurney.

Dave looked at Noa and didn't have to say what he was thinking. Noa responded to the look in Dave's eyes and said, quietly, "He's not going to make it."

Gordon Grant had rushed to their side and heard Noa's diagnosis.

"What do you think it was, Dave, a heart attack?" Gordon asked.

"I guess so. He looked drunk to me, and I could smell rum on his breath. Do you have any idea how many Mai Tai's he had?" Dave inquired.

"No, I'll ask Kulani and see if he knows."

Noa got to his feet and again asked for everyone's attention. Then, in his comforting voice, he announced, "Ladies and Gentlemen, it appears that Mr. Reynolds may have had a heart attack. As soon as we know his condition, we'll let you know. He's on his way to The Queen's Medical Center now."

The party was over. Hypatia rushed over to Noa and asked for directions to the hospital. Tom Butler said he would drive her there. Jennifer remained on the edge of the dining room.

The Grant's and Sullivan's stayed behind while the Club emptied out. As President of the Club, Gordon was concerned that Reynolds might have eaten something that made him sick.

"Jack, you're a lawyer. Do you think I should call the Club's lawyer tonight?"

"Yes, I do, Gordon. Reynolds is a high profile guy, and you can be sure that his lawyers will be calling you tomorrow morning, if not sooner."

"Thanks. I'll get on that right away. Would you excuse me?" Gordon gathered Noa and Georgia and walked toward the Club's office.

"Well, Katherine, what an evening."

"I'm drained, Jack. Let's go home."

They drove back to the Royal Hawaiian and walked silently, arm in arm, to the elevator. As they waited there, Jack hugged Katherine and she held him tight.

It was nearly eleven by the time they entered their apartment. The Maine Coon was curled up, almost in a circle, on one of their living room chairs. He stirred as they walked in, stood up and yawned, let out a mild chirp, then resumed his lounging position on the chair. Katherine immediately scooped Hugo up and kissed his head. Hugo responded by licking her nose.

"I think I'll turn on the news to see if they cover it," Jack said.

"It's too late, don't you think?"

"Nothing is too late for TV news these days, especially when Hollywood is involved."

Jack turned on the local news and, sure enough, there was a short segment that showed the front entrance to the Diamond Head Canoe Club. It reported that Derek Reynolds, the Hollywood producer, had suffered a heart attack and was at The Queen's Medical Center in critical condition.

Jack turned to Katherine, who was flipping through old magazines, and said "I think this guy's in trouble."

"It's so sad," Katherine said. "It was such a happy evening up until that point."

"Yes it was," said Jack.

"I've got it!" Katherine exclaimed. "I found the *People* magazine with a picture of Barbara Franklin standing next to the boy toy we saw at the party tonight."

"Who's Barbara Franklin?" Jack asked. "Do you mean the actress?"

"Yes. Georgia was talking to one of the cast members tonight and she thought he might be Barbara Franklin's boy toy. She thought she'd seen a picture of them in *People*. And, sure enough, here it is. My, my, I'll bet Barbara Franklin has thirty years on him."

"I see what you mean," Jack said, glancing at the photograph. "I guess Georgia's friend likes older women."

"Oh, she was just talking to him, and we both thought we'd seen his picture in *People*. Now," said Katherine with a proud smile, "I can confirm it."

CHAPTER NINE

Jack's alarm went off at six on Tuesday morning. Katherine groaned and asked why he always took the early morning flight to Kona, when he was going to be there all day anyway.

"Oh, sweet one," Jack said, pulling his wife toward him, "I get a lot more accomplished when I'm at the Plantation in the morning. The farm hands see me and talk to me about their work and their lives, and it gives me a better feel for the operation I'm running over there," said Jack.

"I know. I just hate to see you leave this early. It means we spend less time together today, and I don't like that."

"I don't either," Jack said as he turned on the television to hear the local news and weather for the neighbor islands. The weather report was on the screen. It would be a beautiful day on the western side of the Big Island, very sunny and warm with blue skies, a typical day on the Kona Coast of Hawaii. Then the morning show shifted to breaking news.

"We just learned," the newscaster announced, "that Hollywood producer Derek Reynolds has died. We reported late last night that Mr. Reynolds apparently suffered a heart attack while attending a cast party at the Diamond Head Canoe Club. He was producing a film here on Oahu and flew in from Los Angeles last weekend to check on its progress and attend a party for the cast."

"He bit the dust, Katherine," Jack said, sitting down on the foot of their bed.

"What a shame," Katherine added. "That will probably change my morning. Hypatia and Martha couldn't possibly stop by under these circumstances."

"I wouldn't think so. I'm going to jump in the shower. Would you listen for more news? They didn't say what the cause of death was. I hope the Club didn't serve him any bad food."

"Oh, come on, Jack, we eat there all the time. The food is excellent, and the chef couldn't be more careful."

"I know. I'm just thinking of Gordon and how concerned he was last night."

"Why was he worried? He eats at the Club more often than we do."

"Gordon is worried because of that incident on Maui, where a restaurant inadvertently served a reef fish contaminated with ciguatera," replied Jack.

"What is ciguatera?"

"It's a toxin that's sometimes present in fish that swim around reefs and feed on the organisms there. It's very harmful to humans."

"Do you think the Club served any reef fish with ciguatera last night?" asked Katherine.

"I doubt it. As you said, the chef knows what he's doing. But that's why Gordon was so concerned last night. It was a rather sudden event," Jack said.

"Most heart attacks are, Jack."

"That's just it, Katherine, the cause of death hasn't been identified. The news reports are still calling it an apparent heart attack. I'll bet Gordon is beside himself this morning."

"But, Jack, if the fish was bad, Derek wouldn't be the only one who got sick."

"You're right, but I better call Gordon on the way to the airport."

Jack dressed quickly, kissed Katherine, patted Hugo on the head, grabbed his Panama hat, and ran for the stairs down to the fifth floor. When he reached the elevator and the doors opened, he saw Richard Stanley peering in the elevator's mirror, adjusting his tie.

"Good Morning, Mr. Secretary," Jack said cheerily. "And how do you feel on this fine Navy day after a good night's sleep?"

"Thanks to you, Jack, I feel remarkably well. I did exactly as you said. I stayed up till a little after eleven, which, I might add, was not easy. It was four in the morning for me. And I pretty much slept straight through until about six Hawaii time. Then, I got up, listened to the news, and had breakfast in the Surf Room. So I'm ready for anything the Pacific Fleet throws at me today."

"Good for you."

"Jack, I saw on the news that the producer at last night's party died. What happened to him? Did he have a heart attack?" Rich asked.

"I saw the same news you did. I don't know what happened to him."

"He looked and sounded plastered to me," Rich said.

"No question about that."

"Well, I know from my days as a prosecutor that they'll do an autopsy on him this morning," Rich said. We'll know soon enough what caused his death."

"So you were a prosecutor too?" Jack asked.

"I told you we have a lot in common. We've got to get together while I'm out here."

"I agree." The elevator door opened and they stepped out into the lobby where two Naval Officers in white uniforms, one with four gold stripes on his shoulder boards, waited for Richard Stanley.

"Good morning, Mr. Secretary," the Navy Captain said to Rich.

"Good morning, Captain. I'd like you to meet Jack Sullivan, a former Naval Officer who lives here at the hotel and is a friend of mine."

"Good morning, sir," the Captain said to Jack.

"Good morning, Captain." Jack mused at how infrequently he had seen officers of that high a rank during his days on the Destroyer.

"Rich, I'm going to Kona today on business but I'll be back tomorrow. Why don't we meet for dinner at La Mer in the Halekulani at eight?"

"I'll look forward to it, Jack. See you then."

Rich got into the right rear seat of a four-door white sedan with "U.S. NAVY" in blue letters on each of the front doors. Jack thought this was a nice way to travel and wondered whether he had missed something during his own Navy experience.

Jack took H-1 to Honolulu International Airport's Interisland Terminal, parked his car, and walked to the gate. When he reached it, he saw the back of a familiar figure, his companion on many flights between Oahu and the Big Island of Hawaii. It was Stanton Char.

"Stanton, good morning," Jack said.

"Jack, I thought I might see you this morning. And how is Katherine?"

"She's fine, although we're both a little frizzed out after what happened at the Club last night."

"Were you there when Derek Reynolds died?" Stanton asked.

"I don't think he actually died at the Club. But he did keel over and pass out there."

"Yes, I heard about it on the news this morning," Stanton said. "They didn't specify where he died. Typical superficial television coverage, I guess."

"I guess," said Jack.

"So, Jack, how's the coffee business treating you?"

"Pretty well, and due in no small part to the wisdom you have graciously provided me over the last few months."

"It's a complex business, Jack, and I'm happy to help a colleague, even if you are a competitor," Stanton said, smiling as they boarded the aircraft. "In fact, I'm testing out a new technology today that you may be interested in. I'm using a UAV, an unmanned aerial vehicle, to take color video of my orchards that will show where the red, yellow, and green fruits are, so I can direct my labor force right to the red fruits that are ripe for picking."

"I don't think you have to worry about competition from me, Stanton. Your coffee plantation dwarfs mine, and I don't have enough land to make a UAV worth the investment."

"Give it some thought, Jack, but you do have an advantage over me. When tourists come to the island, they want to visit small plantations. They're easier to see and they don't take much time away from the beach. Your plantation is closer to the hotels, and the tourists can see it in a half-hour. Mine requires a longer car ride from the Kohala Coast hotels and a larger investment of time for the tour."

"You are a very generous man," Jack replied.

"Plus you own one of the Big Island's premier coffee properties that has consistently turned out high quality beans, with the exception of that unpleasant period when the dotcommers thought they knew how to run a coffee plantation."

Jack smiled and leaned back in his seat. Derek's death was intruding on his thoughts of the coffee business, but he blocked it out and returned to his conversation with Stanton. He and Stanton had become friends for reasons beyond their common endeavors on the hillsides of Kona. Stanton, too, had served in the Navy. He was a graduate of the Naval Academy who had returned to his birthplace to do good and, in the process, had done well. As the plane landed after the half-hour flight, Stanton asked Jack how long he would be staying on the Big Island.

"I'm going to stay overnight and take a late afternoon flight back to Oahu tomorrow," Jack said.

"So am I. Why don't we have dinner tonight?"

"I'd love to."

"Meet me in the dining room of the Poinciana at eight?"

"I'll be there."

Putting his Panama hat on as protection from Kona's enveloping sun, Jack walked down the airliner's stairway to the warm tarmac below and looked toward the several, low one-story brown buildings at Kona International Airport. He spotted Keoni Campbell, his plantation manager, standing just inside the gate.

"Good morning, Mr. Sullivan," Keoni called as Jack approached.

"Good morning, Keoni, how are you?"

"I couldn't be better. The weather is perfect, and everyone showed up for work on time," Keoni said with a smile.

As he shook Keoni's hand, Jack turned back toward the aircraft and beckoned Stanton Char to join him and Keoni.

"Stanton, I must thank you again for recommending Keoni to me. I couldn't run this operation without him," Jack said.

"Keoni's the best coffee man on this island, and I've tried many times over the years to hire him away from his various employers, with the exception of you, of course."

"Please tell Lokelani and your children that I said hello. I assume they are all fine," said Stanton to Keoni.

"They're all healthy, Mr. Char, and will be happy to hear from you."

Stanton's driver then approached, and Stanton said goodbye.

"He's a wonderful man," Jack said to Keoni. "How come you didn't take him up on his offers?"

"He is a great man," Keoni responded. "Mr. Char has been a leader on this island for a long time. He grew up in Hilo on the wet side of the island and was a star at everything he did. When he won an appointment to the Naval Academy, it was as if every father and mother on the Big Island were his parents. Everyone was so proud of him. But I prefer to work on small farms; I don't like the big operations."

"Well, I'll be forever grateful to him for introducing me to you, Keoni."

"I knew that if Stanton liked you, I would too," Keoni said as they walked out of the terminal to a green Jeep Cherokee with the words 'Kailua Plantation' in white letters on each front door.

They drove south along Queen Kaahumanu Highway for nearly a half-hour until they reached the town of Kailua-Kona, a small tourist town on the western coast of the Big Island, and then turned off the main highway and drove along less developed roads until, a few miles later, they reached Kailua Plantation. There, they turned right into the gravel driveway that led to the office and, a little farther along, to the Sullivans' green plantation-style house.

The farm occupied one of the most beautiful sites on the Kona Coast. Set on a volcanic hillside, it looked down on verdant hills and valleys undulating like green ocean swells that eventually broke as waves on the black sand beach nearly two thousand feet below. The sun shone brighter here than Jack had seen anywhere else on earth, and this location, with its volcanic soil and nightly rains guaranteed by the elevation, followed by brilliant sunshine each morning and protective clouds each afternoon, ensured the quality of Kailua Plantation's coffee beans.

"Would you like to start with a look at the condition of the trees?" Keoni asked Jack.

"I would, Keoni, and I'd like to talk with our guys along the way."

"Certainly."

Keoni led Jack to the orchard of coffee trees that produced the primary cash crop of Kailua Plantation. Along the way there were big-leafed banana trees, colorful lemon and lime trees, and a sprinkling of mango and papaya trees.

The coffee beans begin their lives on tropical evergreen shrubs known as coffee trees. Jack laughed to himself, remembering his reaction when he first laid eyes on these bushes and thought he was in the wrong place. Fortunately, Keoni quickly assured him that those tall shrubs were indeed the real deal — coffee trees that grow only on the sides of mountains between the Tropic of Cancer and the Tropic of Capricorn, where the Big Island was located.

Jack enjoyed inspecting these cheerful, eight-foot high bushes with their broad green leaves and branches marked by clusters of red fruit that looked like cranberries, although everyone referred to them as cherries. But his chief concern was the inside of their pit-like seeds which, after harvesting, processing and roasting, became Kona coffee beans.

He was also mindful of the limited capacity of coffee trees. Each new coffee tree had to grow for five years before it could produce the full bounty of its capacity and, even then, it could only produce enough beans each year to generate one pound of roasted coffee. Nevertheless, as Jack knew when he purchased Kailua Plantation, coffee ranks second only to oil in the volume of commodities traded around the world.

Jack and Keoni stopped to rest on a slope during their walk through the farm, and Jack took in the view. The orchards at Kailua Plantation traced orderly green lines across the black volcanic soil that covered the lower slopes of Mount Hualalai. While the Plantation's elevation of two thousand feet was modest in comparison with the four to six thousand feet in the coffee-growing regions of Central America and East Africa, its location on the volcanic Kona Coast guaranteed porous and fertile soil, the essential natural resource required to produce comparable coffee.

"These trees are in great shape, Keoni. Now, all we have to worry about is Kona coffee maintaining its niche in the world market."

"No problem there, Jack. Kona beans always deliver the mild taste most coffee drinkers want."

The coffee beans that emerged two weeks after they had been plucked from Kailua Plantation's trees and processed, now called green coffee, were about three-eighths of an inch long and grayish-green in color and would be shipped to coffee brokers in San Francisco and New York. The Plantation also roasted green beans for sale throughout the Hawaiian Islands, to visiting tourists, and to Kona coffee-lovers around the world who purchased roasted beans from the Plantation's website.

As Jack and Keoni neared the roasting shed at the end of their tour, Keoni turned to Jack.

"I'm going to roast some beans this morning, Mr. Sullivan. Do you have time to join me?" Keoni asked.

"Absolutely."

Roasting is as much art as science. Fortunately for Jack, Keoni Campbell was a master roaster as well as an experienced farm manager. He knew instinctively when to stop roasting the Plantation's green beans so that their acidity, body and aroma were at their peak.

"Do you ever roast beans beyond ten minutes?" Jack asked.

"Not often. At twelve minutes, what they call the 'Vienna roast' level, the body of the coffee starts to outweigh its acidity. To go to the fourteen-minute 'Italian' and fifteen-minute 'French' roasts, you've really got to have hard and dense beans from higher elevations like Guatemala Antigua beans. I don't want to produce coffee that knocks the socks off the consumer.

I'm looking for that mild and fruity taste people associate with Kona beans."

Just then, Jack's cell phone rang. "Jack, I saw Hypatia this morning."

"So she came by your shop after all."

"Yes, she and Martha and Georgia were here at 10:30, just as we had planned."

"Was she upset?" Jack asked.

"Not particularly, but she did tell me that Jennifer blew up at Derek last weekend when they were at The Poinciana Hotel."

"Really?" Jack replied. "Stanton Char invited me to join him there for dinner tonight."

"Hypatia said she was completely embarrassed. It happened during dinner in the dining room. Her sister got into a major shouting match with Derek."

"That dining room is always so quiet. It must have stunned the guests," Jack said.

"Fortunately, there weren't too many. Hypatia said only a few other tables were filled when it happened."

"Well, she won't have to worry about him anymore," Jack said.

"No, she won't," Katherine replied. "Did you talk to Gordon?"

"No, I decided to wait until I got here. Maybe I should talk to Dave before I call Gordon," Jack said.

"I think you better, Jack, because you know Gordon will ask your advice."

"You're right," Jack said "I'll call Mc Neil first."

"I've got to run, Jack. Call me later."

"Bye baby. Keoni, the next time you roast beyond ten minutes, save me some. I'd like to try it. I'm going up to the house and make some marketing calls."

The house was an old plantation-style place in the Hawaiian tradition. It was one story, made of wood, painted dark green, with white shutters and a wrap-around porch. The front porch looked out on the Pacific, and the back porch faced the orchard. Inside, the mahogany floors were covered with oriental rugs, and the living room was filled with overstuffed furniture upholstered in warm tropical colors and prints. Named "Hale Kai," the house offered a quiet refuge from the frenetic pace of Honolulu.

Jack did most of his work on the Plantation from this house and left the farm's office to Keoni, who managed the growing, harvesting, washing, drying, and roasting of coffee beans and the Plantation's retail sales business.

Jack was trying to develop new markets for his coffee beans. He wanted the finest restaurants on the mainland to serve his coffee, brewed in the French Press fashion at the table, an elegant way to serve coffee that had not yet made it to many restaurants outside Hawaii. Jack wanted to change their menus to include Kona as well as espresso coffee. He had struck a strategic alliance with a glass manufacturer who made excellent French Press beakers and, together, they contacted chefs and restaurant managers on both coasts and in the midwest and sought to persuade them to supplement their current coffee selection with Kailua Plantation beans and French Presses.

After twenty cold calls to restaurants on the mainland, Jack walked back to the farm's office and told Keoni, "I'm going into town to see that guy who makes hula lamps. Katherine has wanted one ever since she first saw them, and I thought I might bring one back for her tomorrow."

"Make sure you get the kind whose hips swivel. They're the real ones," Keoni said.

"I wouldn't think of getting any other kind. And Keoni, I'm having dinner with Stanton Char at The Poinciana Hotel tonight.

"Try the opakapaka, Mr. Sullivan, it's excellent."

"It'll be either opakapaka or ono, Keoni, you know me."

"You can't go wrong with either one. By the way, they had some trouble up there over the weekend. Some loudmouth from Los Angeles got out of hand at dinner on Saturday night. The maitre'd is a friend of mine and he thought he was going to have to call the police."

"I heard about that. The guy was Derek Reynolds, the Hollywood producer. He died today in Honolulu."

"Did somebody shoot him?" Keoni asked. "With a temper like his, I can see how it could happen."

"You mean he had a short fuse?"

"He was explosive. The way my friend described it, he just started screaming at this young woman, using language that was way out of order."

"He made quite a scene at a party in Honolulu last night too," Jack said.

"My friend will be at the restaurant tonight. His name is Emmett. Ask him about it."

"Maybe I will, if I get a chance."

Jack climbed into the 1969 Camaro convertible that he kept on the Plantation and drove out of the farm toward the town of Kailua-Kona. Suddenly, his cell phone erupted with the short ring that signaled receipt of a voicemail message. Jack was wryly mystified at technology that permitted him to receive the message but had not allowed him to receive the actual call, even though his cell phone had been turned on all day and he had earlier received a call from Katherine.

Jack looked at the face of the phone to see the source of the incoming message. It was Dave McNeil's office at Police Headquarters in Honolulu. A somber-toned McNeil asked Jack to call as soon as possible. Jack was certain of one thing. Dave was not calling to talk about golf or paddling.

Jack immediately pulled onto the shoulder of the road, stopped the car, and called McNeil.

"Dave, Jack," he said as the familiar voice answered the call on the first ring. "What's up?"

"I'm not sure yet, Jack, but we got the results of the autopsy. Derek Reynolds didn't die from a heart attack induced by high living and too many Mai Tai's."

"What did the autopsy show?"

"It's what it didn't show, Jack. There was no evidence of the kind of damage to the heart muscle that you see after a typical heart attack."

"So what caused his death?"

"We don't know. The toxicology results haven't come back from the lab yet. They'll tell us what was in Reynolds' blood, in his stomach, in his bladder, the usual," Dave explained.

"When will you have them?"

"The lab says we'll have them first thing tomorrow morning."

"Have you told Gordon yet?"

"No, I haven't and that's why I called. I thought I should wait until I have the toxicology results. I don't want to flip him out. Do you agree?"

"Yes, I do. He was worried last night. All he could think about was that ciguatera incident on Maui last year."

"That's why I called you, Jack. I wanted to see if you agreed with me about waiting to tell Gordon what we know so far."

"I do agree, Dave," Jack said. "At this point, you don't know enough to do anything other than scare the hell out of him."

"Thanks, old buddy. When do you get back?"

"I'll be home tomorrow afternoon, but feel free to call me here. It'll be a pleasant break from arguing with condescending French chefs and know it all restaurant managers about the relative merits of Kona and espresso coffee."

"I'll call you when I get the lab results."

Jack sat in his car, thinking about what Dave had just told him. He wasn't surprised to learn that Reynolds had not died of a heart attack. He had seen Reynolds collapse and noticed that he didn't clutch his chest or grab his left arm in pain or even cry out. Reynolds had only hesitated in the middle of his speech, looked puzzled, and then collapsed in a heap. Jack hoped that these were not the symptoms of ciguatera poisoning.

CHAPTER TEN

The artisan who had designed and cast the hula lamps was very happy to see Jack. At $1,000 a lamp, he didn't sell very many, but he regarded each of them as a work of art. He had performed a valuable service for tourists and Hawaiians alike by bringing these quintessential symbols of Hawaii back to life. Cast in bronze in the shape of a Native Hawaiian woman with a silk-thread skirt hanging on hips that swiveled at the flick of a switch and crowned with hand-painted lampshades depicting scenes in the islands, the lamps brought back Old Hawaii in a way that no modern souvenirs could. Katherine had seen them on their first visit to the Big Island and tracked down the craftsman who made them.

"I'm ready to do it," Jack said, breaking into a broad grin.

"I knew you'd be back to close the deal," the craftsman replied with a smile.

With the lamp and shade safely secured inside packing crates, Jack drove back to the Plantation, thinking about his conversation with Dave and wondering what the toxicology analysis would reveal. The lights were still on in the office, and Jack waved to Keoni as he drove past. Some of the farmhands were rolling the drying platforms into the shed that provided cover from the nightly rains so the beans would remain dry until the platforms were rolled back out into the sunshine the next morning.

Jack showered and put on a bright blue Aloha shirt that featured pineapples and the Hawaiian island of Lanai, another of his favorites. He got back into the Camaro and drove north on Queen Kaahumanu Highway toward the luxury hotels of the Kohala Coast, forty-five minutes away. These hotels were worlds in themselves. The tourists who stayed in them rarely left the hotel grounds, which were set back miles from the main highway. Reaching them required a ten-minute drive west through desolate black volcanic rock formations so primitive that first-time visitors were convinced that they had taken a wrong turn. When they finally arrived at the hotel, they were startled by the green grass, vivid tropical flowers, and tall and full palm trees — a tribute to landscape architects and fresh water irrigation systems.

Twenty-five minutes later, as Jack passed the Kona airport on his left, he decided to take an earlier flight back to Honolulu the next morning. He missed Katherine and wanted to be around if the news of Reynolds' death was bad for Gordon and the Club. Twenty minutes later, he turned left from Queen Kaahumanu Highway and drove west through the moonscape of volcanic rock fields toward the Pacific Ocean and The Poinciana Hotel.

The Poinciana was the Island of Hawaii's most elegant hotel. Dominated by the warm tones of Koa wood in the furniture, doors, and walls, and accented by oriental carpets, the hotel's common rooms resembled the nineteenth century Iolani Palace that Hawaii's last king, David Kalakaua, had built in Honolulu. The Poinciana Room was widely recognized as the island's best restaurant and the only one that still required gentlemen to wear sport coats. The result was a dignified, quiet atmosphere that guests invariably wished would spread to other restaurants on the island.

"Good evening, Jack," Stanton said as Jack approached the maitre'd, "let me introduce you to Emmett, the best maitre'd on the Big Island."

"And a friend of Keoni Campbell, as I learned today," Jack added, shaking Emmett's hand.

"Keoni told me about you, Jack. I'm very glad to meet you."

"Thank you. Keoni tells me you had quite a dust-up here last Saturday night."

"Did we ever," Emmett exclaimed. "I thought I was going to have to call the police to quiet them down."

"What happened?" Stanton asked.

"Well, it was late and there weren't many people left in the dining room. There were two women and a man at a table in the corner, and I noticed that the man was arguing with one of the women, the younger one, while the older one kept trying to quiet them down. Suddenly, the man erupted like Kilauea. He turned as red as lava and began screaming obscenities at the younger woman. I only learned later who they were."

"Did you call the police?" Jack asked.

"No, there was no need to. The older woman calmed them down, and they left the dining room."

"It must have been a lively bit of entertainment for the Saturday night crowd here," Jack said.

"Not everyone recognized them at first," Emmett went on. "But there was a couple from Honolulu seated across the dining room in the alcove that looks out on the ocean and they told their waiter who they were. Then he told me, and I was shocked. Hypatia Adams and Derek Reynolds are famous. I don't know anything about the younger woman, but she was mad as hell at Reynolds."

"Well, I hope you don't lose any customers as a result," Stanton said with an eye toward the bottom line.

"We were lucky it was late, and we had mostly local regulars and that one couple from Honolulu who come here frequently. You probably know them, Stanton — Sidney and George Lane. I was a little worried about them after I saw them check out on

Sunday morning. When they arrived at the dining room on Saturday night, they told me they'd be staying for five days."

"I do know them," Stanton replied. "Sidney used to be a Hollywood actress who probably knew Derek Reynolds. I'm surprised they weren't sitting together."

"I didn't even see them speak to each other. Maybe the Lane's didn't see the Reynolds party until the shouting started and didn't want to embarrass them," Emmett said.

"Probably." Stanton turned to Jack. "Where would you like to sit, Jack, in the dining room or out on the porch?"

"Let's sit inside tonight," Jack replied, "and let the tourists enjoy that view."

"I agree," said Stanton, "although I never tire of looking at the Pacific Ocean."

"Neither do I. That's one of the reasons we moved out here."

Emmett led Stanton and Jack to the alcove table where Sidney and George Lane had sat on the previous Saturday evening.

"This table offers the best of both worlds. An inside table with a view of the ocean," Emmett said as he pulled the table out to allow Stanton to slide in behind it. The alcove had a clear view of the dining room as well as the ocean.

"I can see how the Reynolds party might not have noticed the Lane's," Stanton said as he leaned back into the red leather banquette whose wings extended out from either side of the curved seat.

"Yes, but the Lane's could easily have seen the Reynolds group," Jack responded.

"Maybe they don't like each other."

"That's probably it. Based on my exposure to him last night, I don't think many people did like Derek Reynolds," Jack said.

Emmett returned and introduced their waiter. As Emmett turned back toward his post at the entrance to the dining room, Jack said, "By the way, Emmett, you won't have to worry about

Reynolds coming back and raising hell here again. He died early this morning in Honolulu."

"How did that happen?"

"I'm not sure. The press reported that he had a heart attack, but the police haven't announced anything official yet."

"Well, I'm glad he didn't die here," Emmett said. "The last thing a restaurant needs is for someone to die after dinner. Reynolds didn't die after eating at a restaurant, did he?"

"Actually, he collapsed after a luau at the Diamond Head Canoe Club."

"I know the chef there. He's one of the best chefs on Oahu," Emmett said.

"I agree," Jack said. "I'm sure Reynolds had some kind of pre-existing condition that surfaced and did him in."

"That's probably right. Hypertension is the silent killer, isn't it? He probably had high blood pressure and it finally got to him."

"Well, enough talk of this," Stanton said. "Let's look at the menu. What'll it be Jack, opakapaka, ono or mahimahi?"

"You mean I'm that predictable, Stanton?"

"Well, even though I see marlin on the menu, my gut tells me that you're an opakapaka kind of guy tonight."

"I do love snapper, whether it's red from the Gulf of Mexico, yellowtail from the Atlantic Ocean, or opakapaka from the Pacific."

"Snapper is an excellent fish, regardless of its home waters," Stanton replied. "But I'm having the marlin. I feel the need for a good steak."

"Do you prefer marlin over ahi?" Jack asked, referring to the Hawaiian name for yellowfin tuna.

"It's a close call, and the outcome usually depends on what else I've had to eat earlier in the day," Stanton said. I had an ahi sandwich for lunch, so I've depleted the tuna stock enough for one day."

They placed their orders, asked the waiter to choose a bottle of sauvignon blanc that would complement opakapaka and marlin, then turned to fishing, their other mutual interest.

"Jack, I'm building a boat here on the Big Island. I want to be able to come over from Honolulu and, on a moment's notice, go fishing. And I want to do it from my own boat, with my own tackle."

"I agree. There's nothing like having your own boat with your own rods, reels and lures. How big is it?" Jack asked.

"It's only thirty feet. I don't want to cruise anywhere. The waters between these islands are too rough for that. I just want to get out to the fishing grounds off Kona and catch a few big ones."

"The Kona Coast really is one of the world's great fisheries. What's the Hawaiian word for it? Is it 'kai lawai 'a'?" Jack asked.

"Very good, Jack. You've been studying our language."

"Just listening carefully. I took Latin in high school, and my father studied Latin and Greek. Growing up, he was always teaching us the classical origins of the English language. The Hawaiian language is similar. It combines words and makes concepts out of them. 'Kai' means the sea and 'lawai'a' means to catch fish. I named our house on the plantation 'Hale Kai,' house toward the sea."

"You're becoming an incurable Hawaiian, Jack."

"I hope so. When will your boat be finished?"

"In about six months. I'll keep chartering boats out of Honokohau Harbor in the meantime."

"Are you going to keep your boat there?" Jack asked.

"I wouldn't keep it anywhere else. The fishing grounds off the Kona Coast are so close to shore, just like the Gulf Stream off Boca Raton and Fort Lauderdale. Hell, you go out two miles from Honokohau, and the big fish are right there."

"I know what you mean. I've paddled out there in a canoe, and some very big fish have swum right under me."

"No question about it. That's why my new boat's only thirty feet long. Just long enough to be comfortable for a half day of fishing off Kona."

"That's enough for me too. If I haven't caught anything after four hours, I'm usually ready to head for home."

"Jack, where do you come down on this debate over the legal definition of 'Kona Blend' coffee?

"Well, I'm surprised the legislature didn't raise the Kona content requirement above the current ten per cent level. That seems a bit low to me. I lean toward 30 per cent, which is more in line with the specialty coffee industry standard."

"This debate that will rage as long as farmers, roasters and blenders are selling Kona coffee. It seems to me that as long as the amount of Kona coffee in the blend is disclosed, there's no harm to the consumer. But I do worry that the lower content rule could dilute the Kona coffee brand and turn off some consumers who may be disappointed with its taste."

"Well, Stanton, at the moment I'm resolving that debate by not selling any of my Kona beans for blending with other kinds of coffee beans. I hope the economics of this business let me continue doing that."

"For the foreseeable future, I think they will, Jack. But those of us who are carrying these larger properties have to sell a significant portion of our Kona coffee for the blend market."

"I knew there was an advantage to owning a small property."

Stanton and Jack finished dinner with their usual discussion of soil conditions, rainfall, the market and the new subject of UAV technology, which Jack agreed to try, and walked together from the hotel to their cars.

As Jack drove south toward Kailua Plantation, he reached for his cell phone and called Katherine.

"Hellooo?"

"Hellooo," Jack mimicked in response. "How was your day?"

"Fine, but I miss you."

"I miss you too, but I've got good news. I'm coming home in the morning."

"Did you get everything done today?"

"Pretty much, but I'm worried about Gordon. I got a call from Dave, and he said the toxicology analysis of Derek Reynolds' fluids would be finished tomorrow morning. He was worried about Gordon too."

"Did Dave give you any reason to worry about the Club?"

"No. I just think I ought to be there if Gordon needs some legal advice. He does use me as a general counsel of sorts. And I've got a present for you. You'll like it."

"What is it?" Katherine asked.

"I can't tell you. It's a surprise."

"Is it red?"

"No."

"Does it sparkle?"

"Not exactly."

"Can you wear it?"

"I'm not answering any more questions. I love you and I'll see you tomorrow morning."

"Good night, Jack. I love you too."

As he pulled into the Kailua Plantation driveway, Jack decided that he had one more task to complete before returning to Honolulu. He wanted to ask Emmett one more question. Bounding up the back steps of 'Hale Kai', he went immediately to the kitchen phone and called The Poinciana Hotel.

"Could you connect me with the Poinciana Room?" Jack asked the hotel operator.

"Certainly."

"This is the Poinciana Room," Emmett's recognizable voice intoned.

"Emmett, this is Jack Sullivan."

"Good evening, sir. Did you leave something here in the dining room?"

"No, I was just thinking of something you said about the Lane's. You mentioned that you saw them check out on Sunday morning."

"Yes, I had just arrived to prepare the dining room for Sunday brunch."

"Did they say anything to you about the scene in the dining room on Saturday night?"

"No, they didn't."

"Did they tell you that they knew Reynolds and Hypatia?"

"No. They didn't mention it when they left the dining room on Saturday night or when they checked out on Sunday morning. I figured they were just being considerate of the hotel staff, not wanting to embarrass us."

"Maybe they were. Thanks, Emmett. By the way, the opakapaka was excellent. I'll bring my wife on our next trip to the Big Island."

"I'll look forward to that, Mr. Sullivan, and if you give me a day's notice, I'll reserve the best table for you."

"I'll do that, Emmett. See you then."

CHAPTER ELEVEN

Jack woke up at 5:30 on Wednesday morning. As he dressed, he watched a thirty-one foot Bertram sport fishing boat, easily identifiable by the graceful slope of its deck from bow to stern, heading out into the Pacific in search of marlin, mahi mahi, ono and ahi. Three miles offshore, the white-hulled Bertram altered course from west to south and, although still close to shore, it already had two thousand feet of dark blue Pacific Ocean beneath it. The sea was calm, courtesy of the nearly 14,000 foot high mountains of Mauna Kea and Mauna Loa and the 8,200 feet of Mount Hualalai, which block the northeast tradewinds from roiling the waters off the island's Kona Coast. The early morning sun cast a rose tint on the white hull and on the surface of the blue water.

Seeing the light go on in Keoni's office, Jack called him and asked for a ride to the airport.

"Good morning, Mr. Sullivan," Keoni said as Jack strode into the Plantation office. "I've got some of Kailua Plantation's limited Special Roast brewing. Would you like a cup?"

"I would, Keoni, thanks."

"How was your dinner?"

"It was excellent. I had the opakapaka, as you predicted, and I met your friend Emmett."

"He's a real gentleman, and the Poinciana Room is lucky to have him," Keoni observed.

"Yes he is and yes it is," Jack said, sipping a mug of the small batch of coffee that Keoni occasionally roasted longer than the Estate, Private Reserve and Peaberry full flavor roasts for which Kailua Plantation was so well known.

"Do we warn people with heart conditions about this stuff, Keoni?"

"It does get you going, doesn't it? This is our strongest roast, Mr. Sullivan. I find it increases my enthusiasm for the day ahead."

"It certainly rivets one's attention."

As they got into the Jeep Cherokee, Jack told Keoni that Emmett had described the scene in the Poinciana Room on the previous Saturday night.

"Was I right?" Keoni asked.

"You were. He painted a picture of an explosive guy."

"That's the way he described it to me, too," Keoni said.

When they arrived, Jack thanked Keoni and ran for the seven o'clock flight to Honolulu. Twenty minutes later, he saw the island of Oahu and was soon looking down on Pearl Harbor, picking out the USS Arizona Memorial, the Battleship Missouri, Ford Island, and the Pacific Fleet. In a matter of minutes, they had landed at Honolulu International Airport and Jack was walking through the Interisland Terminal. The lines were beginning to build as tourists arrived for their flights to the neighbor islands of Kauai, Maui, Lanai, Molokai, and Hawaii.

Jack called Katherine from his cell phone, knowing that he would wake her up.

"Is the sun even up yet?" she asked.

"If you take your eye mask off, you'll see that it's another beautiful day in paradise."

"Where are you?"

"I'm leaving the Interisland Terminal. I just came in on the seven o'clock flight. I'll be home in twenty minutes, unless the traffic on Nimitz Highway is worse than it usually is."

Twenty-five minutes later, Jack pulled into the semicircular driveway at the entrance to the Royal Hawaiian. Already parked there was the same white sedan he had seen the previous morning with its contingent of white-uniformed sailors and officers waiting for Secretary Richard Stanley.

"Good morning, Jack," Stanley called from the lobby as Jack walked up the front steps of the hotel. "Are we still on for dinner tonight at the Halekulani?"

"We'll see you there at eight," Jack replied.

When Jack opened the door to their suite, Katherine was just emerging from their bedroom, showered and wearing a pink Royal Hawaiian bathrobe. She ran to him, and they embraced for a long moment.

"What's in the big box?" she asked with a mischievous smile.

"Oh, nothing," Jack said, "just some bags of Kailua Plantation coffee for our friends."

"It looks awfully large for a few bags of coffee."

"Well, we have a lot of friends, Katherine, and they all love our coffee."

"Can I see them?" Katherine asked.

"Sure. But be careful. Sometimes the bags aren't sealed well and they can spill."

As Katherine opened the box, her eyes got big.

"You did it! You bought the hula lamp!"

"It's even got the shade you wanted," Jack replied, pointing to a smaller box.

Katherine hugged Jack again and exclaimed, "Thank you! We've got to try it out right now."

Katherine unplugged the lamp on the end table next to their couch and replaced it with the hula lamp and shade. She turned the light on and then flicked the separate switch that controlled the hula dance movement. Immediately, the bronze hula girl's hips began to move, and the gold silk threads of her skirt swayed gracefully to and fro.

"Fabulous!" Katherine exclaimed.

"I think we're officially part of Old Hawaii now," Jack said.

"No question about it!"

"What's the latest on Derek Reynolds?" Jack asked.

"The morning news just said that the police were still waiting for the toxicology analysis, which I guess is due today."

"That's what Dave told me last night. I'll probably hear from him this morning. And now, would you like some very freshly roasted Kailua Plantation coffee, my dear?" Jack asked.

"I'd love it! I'll get dressed and meet you on the lanai."

Jack selected a more moderate roast than the one he had started the day with. He ground enough beans for four cups of coffee and poured them into the French Press. He then boiled four cups of water, poured it over the ground beans, stirred the grinds into the water, and placed the lid on the beaker. After waiting seven minutes to allow the coffee to brew, he pressed the circular plunger that fit into the top of the lid down to the bottom of the glass. During its short transit, the plunger forced the ground beans through the hot water, and the result was four cups of mild, aromatic Kona coffee.

Their lanai was a narrow balcony outside the living room that looked down on Waikiki Beach. It could only accommodate a small table and two chairs, but Jack and Katherine ate breakfast there every morning. While he waited for her, Jack read the Honolulu Star Advertiser and intermittently looked over the newspaper to watch surfers who were already riding the waves off Waikiki.

He loved to watch the catamarans as they sailed out through the surf, filled with tourists who wanted to see Waikiki from the water. As he watched his favorite yellow catamaran sail over the waves, serenaded by one of its crew blowing a conch shell like a horn to warn swimmers in front of the boat, the telephone in the kitchen rang. Jack ran in from the lanai and reached for the wall-mounted phone.

"Jack, Dave. Can you come down to Headquarters?"

"Can you give me a half hour?"

"Sure."

"Is it bad, Dave?"

"I'm not sure what it is. That's why I want to talk to you before I talk to Gordon."

"I'll be there in thirty minutes."

"Who was on the phone?" Katherine asked as she walked into the living room.

"Dave McNeil. I think he's got the toxicology results, and he wants to talk to me before he talks to Gordon."

"That sounds bad for the Club, doesn't it?"

"I'm not sure yet. Dave didn't give me anything specific. He just asked me to come down to Police Headquarters to talk to him."

"Well, Jack, he wouldn't be asking you to pay him a visit if he had good news for Gordon."

"I think that's probably right, but he was very circumspect. He sounded as if he wasn't sure what the tests had concluded."

"Maybe they weren't conclusive. It wouldn't be the first time that a lab couldn't identify a condition."

"True. I told Dave I'd come down in a half hour, so we better have our coffee now."

"Jack, the lab results won't change if you're ten minutes late. Now let's go back out on the lanai and enjoy a nice breakfast. I've sliced some papaya and lime for you, and the toast will be up in a minute."

"You're right," Jack said as he sat down on the lanai with his wife.

CHAPTER TWELVE

When Jack reached Dave's office, he saw a young woman in a white coat, wearing horned-rim glasses, standing in the door talking to Dave.

"Hey buddy, thanks for coming down," Dave said, extending his hand. "Jack, this is Doctor Julia Wong, the toxicologist who's come over from the State's Department of Health."

"Good morning, Doctor. Nice to meet you," Jack said, wondering what he was about to hear.

"Good morning, Jack," said Dr. Wong.

"Jack, I asked Doctor Wong to join us, because she can explain the results of the toxicology analysis better than I can."

"I doubt that, Dave," Dr. Wong said with a smile. "I've seen you explain crime scenes in court that were more complicated than my work."

Dave blushed and motioned to Jack and Doctor Wong to sit down at the conference table in his office.

"What's the diagnosis, Dave, or should I ask the Doctor that question?" Jack inquired.

"Jack, this is as strange a case as I have ever seen in all my years on the police force."

"Is it a case?" Jack asked.

"It is now."

"What do you mean?"

"Let me ask Doctor Wong to explain what the toxicologists found when they analyzed the fluids in Reynolds' system."

"Jack, how familiar are you with toxicology?" Dr. Wong asked.

"I'm reasonably familiar with the field. I was a prosecutor for a few years and handled medical cases where toxicology played a role as part of the evidence."

"So you know that, as part of an autopsy, we take a look at the fluids in the deceased's body at the time of death," the doctor explained.

"Yes, I know that."

"Well," the doctor continued, "when we examined the fluids in Derek Reynolds' system, we found much of what we expected. His blood, for example, was typical for a man of his age and physical condition. And his stomach contained remnants of the food he had consumed at the luau, all of which were tested and found to be free of contaminants."

"So, you didn't find any trace of ciguatera?"

"No, we didn't," Dr. Wong said. "The fish he ate was fine, as were the meats, fruits and vegetables we also tested."

"Well, that's great," Jack exclaimed. "Gordon will be relieved. I know he was very concerned about the possibility of ciguatera poisoning because of that recent incident on Maui."

"That incident had one very beneficial effect, Jack," said Dr. Wong. "It raised the consciousness of every seafood wholesaler, every chef, and every restaurateur in Hawaii. There hasn't been an instance of ciguatera poisoning since."

"So, should we call Gordon now and give him the good news or, as I suspect, is there another finding from the toxicology analysis that will give him heartburn?" Jack asked.

"Good choice of words, Jack. Let the doctor continue."

"Jack, this kind of analysis lets us eliminate many of the possible causes of death. When we tested the fish in Reynolds' stomach, we found there was no contamination from ciguatera or anything else. We moved from one thing to another, testing each to determine if it was a possible cause of death."

"And you found that all the food he ate from the luau was fine," Jack said.

"That's right."

"What did you test next, Doctor?" Jack asked, adding, "I feel like I'm in trial conducting a direct examination."

"I knew you'd enjoy this, Jack", Dave said.

"We tested the fluids that we found in Reynolds' stomach and bladder next," Dr. Wong said.

"If I had to venture a guess, I'd say it was mostly Mai Tai's," Jack said.

"You're right. His blood alcohol level was quite high, way above the level that would have made him unable to drive a car legally. The findings concerning his stomach and bladder fluids were consistent with that blood level. He had consumed quite a bit of rum in the immediate period before his death."

"Well, I know they call it Demon Rum and that it can give you one hell of a headache, but I didn't think it could kill you," Jack said.

"It can't," Dr. Wong said, "at least not in its normal state."

"Was there something wrong with the rum?" Jack asked.

"No. The rum itself, or should I say rums, because there was more than one kind, as you would expect in a Mai Tai, were fine."

"Is this headed where I think it is?" Jack asked, looking at Dave.

"Keep going, Doctor," Dave said.

"When we analyzed the stomach fluids, we found another substance that, quite frankly, stumped us for a while," Doctor Wong said.

"What was it?" Jack asked the doctor.

"It was an extract from a plant or a shrub; we found remnants of bark in the fluid. It was a very toxic substance."

"So how did this extract get into his body? Or, to put it in lawyerly terms, what was the pathway that led to his exposure to the extract?"

"Before we get to that, Jack, let Dr. Wong tell you more about the substance they found in Reynolds' stomach," Dave said.

"We found a very high concentration of this fluid," Dr. Wong said, "and it's poisonous to humans."

"Do you think someone poisoned Reynolds?" Jack asked.

"Tell him more about Hawaiian plants, Doctor," Dave said.

"Jack, many plants in Hawaii are poisonous. Most people don't realize that there are lots of plants in parks and gardens that, while attractive to look at, are extremely toxic if eaten. A common example is Oleander. I've seen Oleander growing near private homes where it's used to provide cover and privacy. But if you eat it, Oleander is quite toxic. Some children recently roasted marshmallows and hot dogs on Oleander branches and became very ill."

"I didn't know that," Jack said.

"Neither did I," Dave added.

"And I sense that you think someone deliberately put this fluid in something Reynolds consumed?" Jack said, looking at Dave.

"I do, Jack, but I want you to hear more about it, so you'll understand why I think that."

"What makes you think this fluid was intentionally given to Reynolds to cause his death?" Jack asked.

Dave looked at Dr. Wong and nodded, signaling her to continue.

"The concentration and amount of the fluid were high and substantial. Someone pressed a lot of fluid from the leaves and branches of a very toxic plant. And that fluid was bound up with the contents of the Mai Tai."

"Do you think someone who knew about poisonous plants put it in one of Reynolds' Mai Tai's?" Jack said, looking at Dave.

"Yes, I do," Dave replied.

"Do you agree, Doctor?" Jack asked.

"I do. Most of the contents of Reynolds' stomach and bladder were fluids, Mai Tai components. He must have just nibbled at the luau. And we in the Department of Health have a fair amount of experience with the effects of poisonous plants on humans, because there are so many of them here in the islands."

"Do people regularly chow down on them?" Jack asked.

"You'd be surprised. We have two typical consumers. The first are children who simply don't know better and eat whatever they see in the garden or the park. The second are teenagers who hear you can get high from certain plants. They consume them in all kinds of ways, including making tea from them."

"What plant or shrub did the fluid in Reynolds' stomach come from?" Jack inquired.

"We don't know yet."

"Why not?"

"We're familiar with the properties of the common poisonous plants like Oleander and can easily identify them, but there are a great many others out there that we may not see in a lifetime. This may be one of them. We're working on it."

"How soon do you think you'll have it nailed down?" Jack asked.

"I can't say," the doctor replied. "We've put as many resources on it as we can spare but we have many other responsibilities. I hope to get an answer soon."

"So, what's this got to do with me, Dave?" Jack asked.

"Well, I thought you might be the best person to explain to Gordon where we are in this investigation. I know he consults you on legal matters and so I thought you could explain the investigative process to him.

"And I could also help you avoid a sticky wicket since you are a good friend of Gordon's and you will be conducting the investigation of what appears to be a murder at the Club of which he is President and you are a member," Jack pointed out.

"Precisely. I knew you'd understand."

"I'll do it. But you'll owe me one for this. I'm thinking at least three rounds of golf at your club," Jack said with a smile.

"You bring the cigars and it's a deal," Dave said.

"Deal," Jack replied. "It was very nice to meet you, Doctor," he said to Doctor Wong.

Jack left Dave's office and walked back to his car, shaking his head.

CHAPTER THIRTEEN

Jack climbed into his Jeep and headed for the Diamond Head Canoe Club, looking forward to a run in Kapiolani Park and a jaunt in his outrigger canoe. He made a beeline for the locker room, changed quickly, and walked back out through the garage to Kapiolani Park across Kalakaua Avenue from the Club's entrance.

The park supplied Jack with a peaceful retreat on this otherwise troubling day. Mothers walking with their children stopped to spread blankets for early lunches. A few other runners circled the park, and a small group of men and women practiced yoga in the bright sunshine. Pairs of Common Myna birds swooped and zoomed like fighter jets, the white swaths on each brown wing flashing like military insignia as they flew by. The scene had a calming effect on Jack as he set out on the two-mile preface to his paddling workout.

Running always cleared Jack's head. When he was trying cases, he invariably reserved time in the evening for a run. It was then that he thought of points he could make the next day and refined his strategy in light of the way the day's evidence had played to the judge and the jury. Frequently, he would develop new ideas by the beginning of the second mile.

As he ran, Jack reconstructed the events of Monday evening. First, he categorized the various groups of people who were present at the Club during the party. There were the Club's employees — a most unlikely source of malefaction. There was the Hollywood group: the cast of the movie and those involved in its production. Hard to say how each of them felt about Reynolds, but it wasn't likely that they wanted to murder him midway through the filming. There were some local public officials and Navy people, but Jack doubted they knew or cared much about Derek Reynolds before that evening. Finally, there was the local social group, some of whom had known Reynolds previously and had little good to say about him. Most of them, however, seemed to be pretty benign on any issue other than a proposed increase in Club dues.

As he started around the park for the second time, Jack applied the classic formulation for solving crimes. Many people at the party had the opportunity, just by being there, to put something in Reynolds' drink. Several of those present may have had a motive, in light of the way Reynolds treated people professionally and personally. But only one of those had obtained the means and placed the extract from a poisonous plant in Reynolds' drink. Thus, Jack concluded the solution to this crime lay in finding the means, and the best place to start looking for it was the Bishop Museum, which had books on every aspect of Hawaii, including its plant life.

His run completed, Jack walked back across Kalakaua Avenue and cut through the parking garage to the Club's locker room where he changed into his bathing suit. He then walked out to the canoe storage racks, lifted his canoe from its rack, and walked down to the unusually deserted beach.

After placing his canoe on the wet sand, Jack dove into the ocean to cool down after his two-mile jog. The Pacific was warm and salty and its waves massaged his tired legs as he took long, slow strokes out to the end of the seventy-five foot long jetty. Jack floated on his back to relax and gazed at Honolulu's skyline, amazed that such tranquility existed at the edge of a modern American city.

Jack returned to the beach with twenty fast and powerful strokes and placed his canoe in the water. The sea was calm as a lake, and he paddled easily alongside the jetty and through the reef. He decided to take a different trip and headed left toward the Diamond Head Lighthouse rather than to the right and Waikiki. The waters near the Lighthouse were rougher than the waters off Waikiki, because the island of Oahu begins to take a turn at that point toward its Windward Shore. Beyond the Windward Shore lies the North Shore with its famous surfing beaches like Waimea and the Banzai Pipeline that draw the world's best surfers to ride Hawaii's biggest waves.

As he paddled southeast, Jack had to work hard to stay clear of the waves and to avoid being pushed into the reef that lay along his left side. It was an exhilarating tour, one that Katherine hated to see him take because of the strong currents and rambunctious waves, but Jack loved it. When he reached the Diamond Head Lighthouse, marked by its red dome and flared white walls, Jack stopped, rested for a minute, then turned his canoe seaward and paddled out for fifty yards before turning right and heading northwest, back toward the Club.

Jack did not think about other things when he was on the water. Paddling in the Pacific required constant attention. The ocean was always moving and changing, impeding one's ability to stay on course and return safely.

Soon, the wind increased, and the waves began to break earlier and more frequently. Jack applied left rudder with his left foot pedal and took more strokes with his paddle to avoid being shoved on to the reef. He worked hard to keep his canoe headed toward the orange windsock on top of the stake that marked the right side of the channel through the reef to the Club's beach.

As he drew closer to the windsock, Jack noticed that there were still no people on the Club's beach. Had the members been spooked by the events that occurred two days earlier? How would they feel when they learned that Reynolds had been murdered there?

Jack reached the windsock and rested for a moment, surveying the approach to the channel through the reef. As he sat on his canoe with the paddle across his legs, Jack saw a dark shadow on the water to his right. But the azure sky was cloudless, its brilliant blue enhanced by the Central Pacific sunshine.

There were no clouds to cast a shadow, so it wasn't a shadow that Jack had seen. The dark form was in the water, not on it, just beneath the surface, only a few feet from Jack as he sat on the canoe's precarious perch.

Jack looked down and saw the form approaching his canoe at a ninety-degree angle. It was brown and at least half the length of his canoe, nearly twice as long as Jack was tall. He froze as he realized that the form was precisely what his instincts had told him it was – a Tiger Shark – but instantly decided that the best way to deal with this most dangerous shark was to act as if he were not phased by it. He paddled parallel to the beach, taking long and smooth strokes as the shark emerged on the other side of his canoe.

As he paddled, Jack imagined the headline in The Advertiser: local coffee plantation owner attacked and killed by Tiger Shark off Waikiki. Just then, as abruptly as the shark had appeared, it vanished. Jack turned his canoe around carefully and took long and deep strokes back toward the windsock. He stretched his torso upward to find the jetty and line it up with the left side of the Surf Hotel so he could run the middle of the channel. Suddenly, Jack heard the sound of an engine behind him, and an outboard motor boat roared by, leaving a wake that threw him off the canoe not far from the place where he had first seen the shark.

The wind and current swiftly pulled his canoe away from him, but Jack maintained a death grip on his paddle. He swam toward the canoe like a man being chased by a shark, which he felt was likely the case, and reached it just as the canoe passed the seaward end of the jetty. Fueled by adrenaline, Jack launched himself like a rocket up out of the water and onto the canoe. Breathing heavily, and rotating on his stomach, he brought both legs on board and sat upright, paddle in hand. Soaking wet and suffused with the joy of a man spared a prehistoric death in the jaws of a sea monster, Jack cursed the driver of the boat and then paddled toward the windsock. When he felt he had reached the midpoint between the jetty and the windsock, he applied pressure to the left foot pedal, turned the canoe straight toward the beach, positioned his canoe between two waves, and dug the paddle into the water repeatedly. As the canoe surfed onto the beach, he relished the luxury and security of the sand between his toes.

Forgoing the weights, Jack took a steam and a shower and decided to reward himself with a grilled mahimahi sandwich on the Club's Lanai. He walked through the bar on his way to the Lanai and saw Kulani getting ready for the lunch crowd. Jack waved and asked how he was doing.

"I was doing pretty well, Mr. Sullivan, until midnight last night," Kulani said.

"What happened?"

"I was driving home after cleaning up and closing the bar, and some guy tried to run me off the road. Nearly killed me."

"Where did it happen?" Jack asked.

"I live out near K-Bay," Kulani said, referring to the Marine Corps Air Station at Kaneohe Bay on Oahu's Windward Shore, "and I was driving near Kailua Beach when this maniac comes up from behind and tries to pass me, but instead hits me and pushes me off the road. My car is totaled."

"Are you okay?"

"I'm fine, but my car is ruined."

"Did you get a look at the driver?"

"Only briefly, when the car was next to me. I looked over just before I got hit. I told the police."

"What did the driver look like?"

"A haole for sure but with a hat on and a scarf around the neck like you see in those old movies. And a turned-up collar," Kulani added.

"Young or old?"

"Hard to tell. But the eyes, they were on fire. They looked at me as if they were mad at me."

"Was it a case of road rage?"

"If it was, I didn't do anything to cause it."

"Have you done anything to anybody lately that would make them mad at you?"

"No. This was something else. I've never seen a look as angry as this one. Must have thought I was someone else."

"Did you get the license plate?"

"No, by the time the car passed me, I was off the road and on the beach, just trying to keep control of my car."

"Could you tell what kind of car it was?"

"I told the police it was a Ford Taurus, I think. It looked like the rental cars you see all over the island."

"Well, that shouldn't be too hard for the police to track down," Jack said.

"No, they said they'd go to the rental agencies and try to find it."

"I'm glad you're okay, Kulani."

"Thank you, Mr. Sullivan."

Jack enjoyed a grilled mahimahi sandwich, cole slaw, and two Diet Cokes. Then he decided he was ready to return to the business at hand, still grateful that he had escaped the interest of the twelve-foot Tiger Shark.

CHAPTER FOURTEEN

Jack bounded up the steps of the Bishop Museum with an enthusiasm he had previously reserved for less sedentary activities than research. He waved to the librarian he knew best, Maile Carter, and asked where he could find materials on poisonous plants.

"Where is your interest in Hawaiian coffee plantations taking you now, Jack?" Maile asked.

"This isn't for my farm. It's for a special project."

Maile smiled and pointed to a dark corner of the stacks.

"The botany section is over there. I recommend that you start with general treatises on plants that are native to the Hawaiian Islands. They will lead you to the dangerous ones."

"Are there many of those?" Jack inquired.

"I'm no expert," Maile replied, "but we do get inquiries from time to time, mostly from students who are interested in Hawaiian customs."

"Why would they want to know about poisonous plants?"

"I'm about to exhaust my knowledge of this topic, Jack, but I think you will find that Native Hawaiian customs and traditions include a god with power over sorcery and poison. His name is Kalaipahoa, and his poison came from plants that grow in these islands."

"Well, that gives me a good start, Maile. Thanks," Jack said.

"I'm afraid that's all I know about the subject. You might consult a Hawaiian Healer if you want to pursue it further."

"A what?"

"A Hawaiian Healer," Maile repeated. "They practice herbal medicine. It's called 'la'au lapa'au', and those who practice it use herbs and plants as their medicine. In Hawaiian, 'la'au' means plant and 'lapa'au' means medicine."

"Do you know one of these guys, Maile?" Jack asked.

"The most famous 'kahuna la'au lapa'au' on Oahu is Papa David Wai'hee."

"I thought 'kahuna' meant chief or important guy. And what's with the Papa?"

Laughing, Maile explained the significance of these titles.

"'Kahuna' is the unfortunate victim of colloquialism. Here in Hawaii, it actually refers to someone who is particularly skilled in something, in this case herbal medicine."

"And Papa?" Jack asked. "Is this an affectionate term like Papa Hemingway?"

"Not quite, Jack," Maile explained. "Papa is an honorary title given to an older man who has distinguished himself during his life."

"Could you set up a meeting for me with Papa David?" Jack asked.

"Yes. But I think you should consult him only after you've done your homework here in the library. Papa David will be much more helpful if you're familiar with the subject matter. He's a very intellectual man who has spent his life studying and practicing herbal medicine."

"Okay. Let me get to it," Jack said with a smile. "And, by the way, Maile, do you keep records of the people who come in here to look at your books?"

"Yes. Didn't you sign in?"

"I did."

"Good, then I'm sure whoever you're looking for also signed in."

"Why do you think I'm looking for someone?"

"We Hawaiians are very perceptive, Jack. You expressed a sudden interest in poisonous plants followed immediately by an inquiry about the identity of people who may also have come here to learn about poisonous plants."

"I better get to the stacks before I blow my cover," Jack said laughing.

"CIA or FBI, Jack?" Maile asked with a broad smile.

Jack returned her smile as he walked toward the dark corner and the stacks of books under the category of botany.

Jack surveyed the range of scholarly books about plants that grow in the Hawaiian Islands. Their titles ran the gamut from botanical treatises containing descriptions accompanied by black and white drawings of plants to cultural tomes that explained the roles that plants have played in the social and religious lives of Hawaiians. He took Maile's advice and began with the botanical treatises.

As Jack paged through the descriptions of Hawaiian flora, he was grateful that his physician father had taught him so much about the Latin and Greek roots of English words. Like medicine, the science of botany employs the classical languages to describe and categorize its constituents.

Jack decided to start with Oleander, because Dr. Wong had mentioned it to him. He discovered that this very common ornamental shrub, known to botanists as Nerium oleander, was highly poisonous. The description of its long and narrow green leaves and large pink, white and red flowers belied the fact that consuming any part of them could cause irregular heartbeat, respiratory paralysis, and death.

Intrigued, Jack turned the pages and found the drawing and description of a small tree with narrow, dark green leaves and yellow flowers shaped like a funnel. Known in the world of botany as Thevetia peruviana, this was commonly called the Be-Still

Tree in Hawaii and it was often the cause of fatal poisoning preceded by vomiting and shock.

Paging through the treatise, Jack came upon another common plant known in botanical circles as Solanum sodomeum and colloquially as the Apple of Sodom. It was described as a low weed with thorny leaves, blue flowers, and yellow berries; when consumed, it caused a sudden drop in body temperature, paralysis, tremors, and death in a deep coma.

Another plant he came upon, called Datura stramonium by botanists, was known in Hawaii as the Jimson Weed or Thorn Apple. The treatise described its leaves as dark green on one side and light green on the other, with its trumpet-shaped flowers ranging from white to violet. If consumed, it could cause mania, convulsion and death.

Jack sat back in his chair and reflected on his findings. He wondered how many poisonous plants there were in Hawaii and how long it would take the toxicologists at the Department of Health to identify the source of the fluid that had killed Derek Reynolds. As he reviewed the properties of the poisonous plants he had found, Jack noticed that one common thread ran through their symptoms. Each produced an evident form of trauma such as convulsion, vomiting, and paralysis. Derek Reynolds had not displayed any of these symptoms. He had merely collapsed and, later, expired.

Jack looked at his watch and realized that the afternoon had flown by. In three hours, he had learned enough about the poisonous plants of Hawaii to talk intelligently about them with Papa David. As he walked toward the librarian's desk, Maile smiled at him and beckoned him to her desk.

"I called Papa David for you, and he would be glad to meet with you tomorrow at noon," she said.

"Really?" Jack exclaimed. "That's great, Maile."

"Are you ready for him, Jack?"

"I am. And I've even got some questions for him that the books didn't answer."

Are they medical questions?" Maile asked.

"Yes, they are."

"Good. Papa David loves to talk about medicine. Here's his address. He lives in Haleiwa on the North Shore.

"Thank you very much, Maile. I really appreciate your help."

"My pleasure, Jack. Good luck."

Jack loped down the steps of the red building that housed the Bishop Museum and walked toward his Jeep, convinced that he had just taken the first step on a journey that would ultimately lead to the person who had murdered Derek Reynolds.

CHAPTER FIFTEEN

Jack got lucky on his trip home from the Bishop Museum. The traffic on H-1, which by late afternoon was usually bumper to bumper, was light. Perhaps, Jack thought, Kalaipahoa was looking out for him. He was early enough to visit Katherine at her dress shop in the Halekulani before she closed at 5:30.

As Jack pulled into the Royal Hawaiian driveway, he noticed the white Navy sedan leaving. Richard Stanley's scheduler had wisely left the Assistant Secretary enough time at the end of the day for a swim on Waikiki Beach. Jack left his Jeep with the doorman and walked briskly over to the Halekulani, cutting through the Sheraton Waikiki Hotel that stands between the Royal and the Halekulani.

Jack reached the window of Katherine's dress shop and saw two very elegant Japanese women engaged in animated conversation with Katherine. He always marveled at how well his wife communicated with women from Japan, even though she spoke no Japanese and they generally spoke very little English. A gentle bell rang as Jack opened the door to the shop, and Katherine waved at him and asked him to join the conversation.

"Ladies, this is my husband, Jack. He has a very good eye for fashion."

Smiling, Jack turned to the ladies, "I'm not a professional, but I do have good taste," he said, glancing at Katherine. "And I think I'll know whether your husbands will like these dresses."

Each woman held up the dress she had selected, and Jack nodded his head at each.

"I will take it," the women stated in unison. And with that, they each produced a credit card, concluded their purchases, and left the shop smiling.

"I want to hear about your day," Katherine said. "What happened at Dave's office? Did you talk to Gordon? Where have you been all afternoon? Help me close up and tell me everything while we walk home."

Jack gave her a detailed summary of his day and, by the time they reached their apartment in the Royal Hawaiian, they were both ready for a swim.

"When are you going to call Gordon and tell him what's going on?"

"Right now. I didn't want to disturb him at his office. I thought this might be the kind of discussion he'd want to have in private."

"Smart thinking. Will you join me for a swim?"

"I will, right after I talk to Gordon. Why don't you go ahead down to the beach while I call him."

"Okay, but don't be long. Our dinner reservation at La Mer is for eight o'clock."

"I'll be down in fifteen minutes."

Jack called the Grants' house, and Georgia answered the phone.

"Georgia, this is Jack."

"Jack, you say that every time you call. You know I know your voice."

"Sorry, I keep forgetting your uncanny voice recognition abilities. Have you told Dave Mc Neil about them?"

Laughing, Georgia replied, "No, and now on to far more serious matters. When are we getting together with you and Katherine?"

"How about Friday evening for dinner at the Club?" Jack asked.

"Perfect. I'll put Gordon on, and the two of you can make the arrangements."

Gordon picked up the phone, and Jack detected immediately that his friend was upset.

"Jack, how are you," Gordon asked sharply, the tension evident in his voice.

"I'm fine. How are you doing?"

"Frankly, I'm concerned that it's Wednesday night and I haven't heard from anyone about what caused Derek Reynolds to collapse at the Club on Monday night."

"That's what I'm calling about, Gordon."

"Have you heard something?"

"I have. I talked to Dave this morning, and he asked me to call you. I thought I'd wait until you got home from the office so we could talk privately."

"What is it, Jack? Did the Club serve him some bad fish?"

"No, the Club's food was fine. The toxicology report cleared the fish and all the other food at the luau."

"You waited to tell me that in private?"

"No. There's something else going on."

"What is it?"

"The toxicology analysis found a poison, from a plant, in Reynolds' stomach. It was toxic enough to kill him."

"Do they think somebody poisoned Reynolds at the Club?"

"Yes, they do."

"Holy shit! I've been a member of that Club my entire life, and nothing like this has ever happened before."

"I know. The reason Dave didn't call you, and he feels bad about that, is that he's in charge of the investigation."

"I understand completely. He's doing the right thing. How can I help him?"

"He'll let you know as the investigation proceeds. If this is a typical murder investigation, you'll be interviewed by a homicide detective who reports to Dave."

"Should I alert the Club's board and the employees?"

"No, not until you've met with the detective, which I'm sure will be very soon. You don't want to jeopardize their investigation. Besides, none of this is public yet."

"What are they waiting for?"

"They haven't identified the poison. They know it came from a plant, but they don't know which one."

"Oh hell, there are so many goddamned poisonous plants in these islands, it'll take them forever. They'll lose the murderer if they wait until they identify the plant. What difference does it make anyway? The guy was poisoned. The point is to find out who did it."

"You know, Gordo, that's why you're such a great leader and successful businessman. You know how to cut through the bullshit and get to the bottom line. But the rest of the world, particularly the criminal justice system, doesn't work that way. They are very methodical, which causes them to be slow sometimes, but it usually results in a thorough examination of the facts and conviction of the bastard who committed the crime. I'm going to join Katherine now for a swim before dinner. Call me after you meet with the detective from homicide. And, by the way, we're having dinner at the Club on Friday night. I just cleared it with Georgia."

"Thanks, old buddy. See you then."

Jack's second swim of the day was equally refreshing and all the more enjoyable because Katherine was with him. They swam out clear of the tourists and watched the surfers catch waves on Hawaii's most famous beach.

"You know what job I'd like to have, Katherine?" Jack said, floating on his back. "I'd like to be the captain of the yellow catamaran that takes tourists out through the surf, gives them a whale's eye view of Waikiki, and rides the waves back in."

"Were you a sea captain in an earlier life?"

"I must have been. I'm not kidding."

"Believe me, I know you're not kidding," Katherine laughed as she bobbed on the gentle waves.

"I guess I'll have to settle for practicing law and owning a coffee plantation for now."

"You'd be bored sailing a catamaran back and forth all day long."

"No, I wouldn't. The wind and the waves and the current are different each time you go to sea. Oh sure, there are some similarities, but no two trips would ever be the same. And I haven't even considered the different people I'd take on each trip."

"What would I do? Blow the conch shell? Serve them lunch?"

"How bad would that be? You enjoyed that catamaran trip we took to watch whales off the Big Island, didn't you?"

"I did enjoy that, Jack, because I was a guest and someone else was worrying about the wind and the waves and the whales and, I might add, the lunch."

"I hear you. We better head in and get ready for dinner. Are you excited about La Mer?"

"Yes, I am," said Katherine. "I hope your Navy friend enjoys the restaurant."

"I'm sure he will. Rich is our kind of guy, and he's a long way from home," Jack said as he and Katherine emerged from the surf and walked toward the shower at the edge of the beach.

"Jack, I'm going to run up and get ready. Don't gab too long about fishing with those beach boys at the pool. We only have an hour to get ready and walk over to the restaurant, and you can talk fishing with those guys tomorrow."

"I promise. I just want to find out where they're catching ulua today."

After learning where Oahu's surf fishermen were catching the most prized local sport fish, Jack filed the information in his fishing memory bank. He had been surfcasting as long as he could remember and, under his father's instruction, had become quite adept at it as a boy. Fishing from the beach had always been his favorite way of tangling with denizens of the deep.

"Hellooo," Jack said as he entered their apartment.

Hugo stirred and looked in his direction but didn't move.

"Don't get up, Hugo. I'll just be a minute, old boy."

"Who are you talking to?" Katherine asked from the bathroom.

"Our Maine Coon."

Katherine walked out of the bathroom with her pink robe on. Jack put his arms around her and kissed her and told her that he loved her. She put her head on his chest and told him how perfectly happy she was.

"I'm going to take a very quick shower and I'll be ready in ten minutes," he said.

When Jack emerged from the bathroom, he saw an Aloha shirt hanging on the bedroom closet door. Katherine had chosen a dark green silk shirt with a pattern that resembled the leaves of a small tree.

"That's a perfect shirt for tonight, Katherine."

"Why do you say that?"

"Because I spent the afternoon looking at pictures of leaves on small trees and shrubs that can kill you."

"Well, you won't have to worry about that at La Mer. I'm sure the salads there are safe to eat."

"I just thought you'd want to know that you're psychic."

"Psychic or psycho?" Katherine replied with a laugh.

"The former, my dear."

"Well that's good to know. There's enough of the latter in the world already."

Jack and Katherine arrived at the Halekulani just before eight and walked upstairs to La Mer, where the walls were covered in the cocoa tones of Hawaiian koa wood and the candlelit porch extended out over the Waikiki surf.

"Jack, this really is the most romantic restaurant in the Pacific. Do you remember our first dinner here on our honeymoon?"

"I do. It's been my favorite restaurant since that evening."

David, the maitre'd, recognized the couple immediately and showed them to a table overlooking waves crashing into the seawall twelve feet beneath them.

"Mr. and Mrs. Sullivan, it's so nice to see you. What time will your guest arrive?"

"He should be here any minute, David."

"May I get you cocktails?"

"Yes," Jack said. "We'll each have a Martini. Tito's Vodka and a capful of Tanqueray Gin. No Vermouth. Shaken until very cold. A twist of lemon in each and olives on the side."

Katherine smiled and turned to Jack. "I thought you might have a Bombay Sapphire Martini rather than a Wiki Wiki after the day you've had, Jack. You certainly deserve one after learning about a murder, escaping the jaws of a Tiger Shark, and spending the afternoon reading about poisonous plants that may have been put in a Mai Tai."

"I thought about it, but I'd like to be lucid for the entire evening, and Sapphire decreases that likelihood."

"Yes, but it is made from botanicals. You know, juniper berries, lemons, licorice, and coriander," Katherine said.

"Have you been reading liquor bottle labels recently?"

"No, but there's a bottle of Bombay Sapphire on the drinks trolley just behind your chair," Katherine said with a smile as the waiter arrived with their Wiki Wiki's.

"All the more reason to stick with vodka tonight. I'm going to spend tomorrow afternoon talking about plants."

"Touche', Jack."

Announcing with a smile that "Your prescriptions have arrived," the waiter served their drinks just as Richard Stanley joined them at the table. He was a tall, prematurely gray-haired, handsome man in his late forties.

"Good evening, Rich, let me introduce you to my wife Katherine."

"I'm delighted to meet you, Katherine."

"May I get you a cocktail, sir?" the waiter inquired.

"I'll have a Bombay Sapphire Martini, very dry and very cold, straight up with two olives."

Jack and Katherine burst out laughing and then explained their reaction. In response, Rich smiled.

"Well, I was lucid all day," Rich said, "and, frankly, I need a stiff drink after sitting through all those briefings at Pearl Harbor."

"Were they interesting?" Katherine asked.

"They were, but the jargon nearly did me in."

"What's the problem?" Jack asked.

"These guys drive ships and fly aircraft for a living. They are great guys, terrific leaders and warriors, and very knowledgeable. But they speak their own language, and it doesn't always coincide with the words the rest of us use."

"That trait isn't limited to military officers, you know," said Jack.

"I know and I don't mean to criticize them. But after a day of technical presentations, I need a stiff drink."

"The business boys have their own lingo too," Jack said.

"That's management-speak, their first language," Katherine said.

"Unfortunately, clarity of language is not very important to most people these days," Jack replied. "They're focused on the bottom line — winning a war or making a profit. Descriptions of how they got there or didn't get there are not of much concern to them."

"Well, lawyers are still carrying the banner for clarity in the written and spoken word, although that's about all they're carrying the banner for these days," Rich said.

"Katherine," Jack said with a wry grin, "Rich is a recovering lawyer."

"Good for you, Rich."

"You know, it just got to be ponderous in the last few years. Fundamentally, I wanted to be the guy making the decisions."

"I know what you mean," Jack said. "I always felt it was better to be the guy who made the decisions than the guy who advised the guy making the decisions."

"Gentlemen," Katherine interjected, "we are not going to talk about the law all night, are we?"

"Absolutely not," Rich said. "In fact, I haven't thought about it much since I left for the Pentagon and, so far, I haven't missed it."

"Welcome to Hawaii, Rich," Jack exclaimed as the waiter placed a Bombay Sapphire Martini with two large olives impaled on a toothpick in front of Rich.

"And to Honolulu!" Katherine said happily. "Now, Rich, tell us how you're enjoying life as a political appointee."

"First, let me offer a toast to new friends," Rich said as he raised his glass to the Sullivan's.

"Katherine, I have enjoyed it immensely. Every day has been fascinating. I deal with the broadest range of the most interesting issues that are important to the country, and the people I work with are terrific."

"Do you miss the money?" Jack asked.

"I do, but not enough to leave the Pentagon and return to private practice."

"Are there any parts of it that you don't like?" Katherine asked.

"As surprising as this may sound, given that I'm a political appointee, I don't always like the politics that go along with the job."

"Are you referring to the glad-handing?" Jack asked.

"No, I don't mind meeting people, although it does take some time to get used to being a public figure, meeting hundreds of people and speaking to them. What I don't like is the occasional pressure to make decisions on bases other than the merits," Rich said.

"You mean pressure to make a decision based on political considerations rather than the facts?" Jack asked.

"Precisely. Fortunately, it doesn't happen too often. Unfortunately, when it does happen, it's usually on an important issue."

"That would be hard for me too," Jack said.

"I don't think I could do it," said Katherine. "I'd tell them where they could go."

"They'd probably listen to you, Katherine," Rich said laughing. "But enough of the law and politics, tell me how you two got out here and what you're doing and how you like it."

After ordering a bottle of chardonnay and entrees of marlin, ahi, and opakapaka, the sipped their respective Martini's and talked about their lives. Jack and Katherine regaled Rich with the story of how they had met, married, honeymooned in Hawaii, and decided that their future together should have as much adventure as possible in as beautiful a place as they could find.

"You actually did what most of us only talk about," Rich remarked.

"I would never have had the courage to do it without Katherine," Jack said.

"Nor I without Jack," Katherine added.

"So there really is something to the old saw about marriage that the whole is greater than the sum of its parts," Rich said.

"No question about it" Jack said. "I felt it the moment Katherine let go of her father's hand and took mine on the altar."

"Me too," Katherine said, looking lovingly at Jack.

"I hope I'm as lucky as you two some day," Rich said.

"You will be, Rich. Just hold out for the right one," Katherine said.

"My father always told me that I'd know the right one when she came along, and he was right," Jack said.

"Well, I've certainly had my share of wrong ones," Rich responded.

"Don't get discouraged, Rich," Katherine said. "She could be right around the next corner."

As their entrees arrived, Rich looked at Katherine and said, "I'll take your advice and keep an eye out at that next corner. By the way, it's a shame that Derek Reynolds bit the dust. Did they conclude he had a heart attack?"

"The police haven't issued a statement yet," Jack said.

"Why haven't they? Don't they routinely do autopsies here in Honolulu?"

"Maybe they're being extra careful in this case, because Reynolds was such a well-known person," Jack said, trying not to disclose more than Dave would have liked.

"Well, I guess I'm not surprised that they'd do a thorough autopsy in his case. That was quite a crowd at the party," Rich said.

"What do you mean?" Jack asked.

"Oh, the cast and crew were composed of the usual cross-section of Hollywood types, and there's always at least one of them who finds the need to consume something other than the available legal substances."

"Did you see anyone with drugs in the Club?" Jack inquired.

"No, but I went into the men's room and there was somebody in a stall who sounded as if he was doing something other than merely dropping his drawers or pulling them up."

"Did you see him?" Jack asked.

"No, and I didn't even make the connection until I heard about Reynolds' death."

"Could it have been Reynolds in the men's room?" Jack asked.

"No, I saw him talking to a group of people when I came out of the bathroom."

"Well, I can assure you that it wasn't a member of the Club or an employee of the Club. That kind of stuff does not go on there and would not be tolerated," Jack said.

"I have no doubt. In any event, we'll know the cause of death when they issue the autopsy report," Rich said.

"That we will," Jack responded.

After Kona coffee and macadamia nut ice cream, Rich glanced at his watch. "Well, it's been a wonderful evening, but I'm afraid my car picks me up at seven tomorrow morning for another round of briefings and meetings. I should hit the hay."

"I hope they're less technical than today's round," Jack said.

"They will be. The Navy officer who travels with me asked me how I enjoyed today's briefings, and I told him I found some of them a bit hard to parse. I'm sure he's conveyed that message to tomorrow's briefers."

"Shall we walk back to the Pink Palace?" Katherine asked.

"I'm ready. You know, the Royal is a terrific hotel," Rich exclaimed, "I'm really enjoying it."

"It's also good for the local economy that you're staying here in town, Rich," Jack said, "and you'll get a much better feel for the city than if you were staying out at Pearl Harbor."

"I agree and I want to thank you both for a great evening," Rich said. "I've made two new friends here tonight."

"You have. Let's try to get together again before you return to Washington," Jack said.

"And Rich, she's right around the next corner," Katherine reminded him.

"I'll count on it, Katherine."

They said good night in the lobby, and Jack turned to Katherine and asked if she would take a short walk in the court-yard behind the Royal Hawaiian's lobby.

"Sure. What are you thinking about?"

"Something that Rich said."

"What?"

"He heard somebody doing something in the men's room other than the usual."

"He thought someone might be taking drugs, didn't he?"

"That's what he thought. But that someone could also have been preparing poison."

"Do you think?"

"Why not?"

CHAPTER SIXTEEN

Jack was sitting on their lanai overlooking Waikiki Beach the next morning when Katherine brought him a cup of Kailua Plantation's finest Kona coffee and his favorite breakfast of sliced papaya with a lime and whole wheat toast.

"Thank you, baby," Jack said, drawing his wife close to him and hugging her.

"You're welcome, hubby," she said, sitting down with her coffee and toast.

The Maine Coon lounged at their side, occasionally dropping his head into a bowl of milk and then shaking it to clear the milk from his whiskers, launching drops of milk across the lanai.

"What time do you meet with the doctor?" Katherine asked.

"Noon, and I think he's called a Hawaiian Healer."

"That should be an interesting way to spend Thursday afternoon. What do you hope to learn from him?"

"I want to find out what plant he thinks was the source of the poison that killed Derek Reynolds."

"How would he know that? He hasn't even seen the toxicology report," Katherine observed.

"I'm going to describe the symptoms as I remember them and just see where it goes from there. I'll tell him what kind of guy Reynolds was and who was present at the party. Maybe that will trigger something in his mind."

"Wouldn't it be better to do some more research first?"

"Probably, but Maile at the Bishop Museum called him for me, and I don't think I should pass this opportunity up."

"I agree," Katherine said as she finished her coffee and got up from the table.

"What are you doing today?" Jack asked.

"Hoping that some more ladies like you met yesterday drop by and decide they simply must have something from my shop. And Hypatia said she may come by with Jennifer."

"Really?"

"Yes. Hypatia said she was sorry that Jennifer hadn't been able to come by on Tuesday morning and wanted to bring her by later in the week."

"Why didn't Jennifer join Hypatia on Tuesday morning?" Jack asked.

"Jennifer called her early that morning and said she didn't feel well."

"Has she recovered?"

"I'll find out today if they stop by."

"I wonder whether any other folks who attended the party on Monday night didn't feel well on Tuesday morning," Jack said.

"Do you think someone tried to poison Jennifer as well?"

"No," Jack said, "but I better get going if I want to get to Haleiwa by noon."

Jack and Katherine took the elevator to the lobby where they ran into Peter Dillingham, the manager of the hotel.

"I've been talking with some Old Hawaii hands," Peter said, "and we've come up with the most exciting idea to liven things up around here."

"Peter, people don't come here for excitement," Jack said. "They've got plenty of that back home."

"I don't mean that kind of excitement. I'm going to bring back an Old Hawaii tradition and broadcast a radio show from the Mai Tai Bar."

"That sounds like a great idea, Peter."

"What kind of radio show will it be?" Katherine asked.

"It will feature traditional and contemporary Hawaiian music."

"Thank God. We don't need another talk show on the air waves," Katherine said.

"Exactly. I decided to revive an old radio show format that used to originate from the Moana Surfrider Hotel, known as 'Hawaii Calls'. It was quite popular and heard around the world. Arthur remembers it. But this time we'll broadcast a show on the radio and we'll stream it on the internet."

"Wonderful. We can't wait to hear it, Peter," Katherine said.

"You can not only hear it, Katherine, you can see it,"

Peter replied with a flourish. "I'd like you and Jack to be my guests at the broadcast of the first show."

"We'd love to," Katherine said.

"When's the first show?" Jack asked.

"With luck, next week, if everything goes right."

"What are you going to call it?" Katherine asked.

"'This Is Hawaii'," Peter proclaimed with obvious pride.

Just then, Jack's Jeep arrived at the hotel entrance. He kissed Katherine goodbye and asked Peter to call them as soon as the show's first performance was scheduled.

As Jack drove from Waikiki to McCully Street and then zigzagged through the small streets that led to H-1, he began to think about possible suspects. The most likely, he thought, was someone who held a grudge against Reynolds. It was unlikely that those who had met Reynolds for the first time Monday night would have had enough time to develop any more than a visceral dislike for the man. Jack began to think about the people at the party who had known Reynolds long enough to generate the hatred that must have fueled his murder.

When he passed the exit for Pearl Harbor, Jack smiled as he imagined Richard Stanley sitting in the gray, World War II-era building that served as Pacific Fleet Headquarters, translating his morning briefings. Shortly, the exit for Oahu's second modern highway, H-2, emerged and he bore right in a northwesterly direction toward the town of Haleiwa on Oahu's North Shore. Jack always enjoyed this ride, because the scenery resembled Oahu as it was a hundred years ago when sugar and pineapples drove Hawaii's economy.

Soon, the Waianae Mountains loomed on Jack's left, four thousand feet above the Army base at Schofield Barracks. This part of Oahu was a fertile plain covered by fields of pineapple and sugar cane. These green crops stood in bright contrast against the rust-colored soil that looked like clay waiting to be molded into bricks. Fire and smoke in a distant part of the field signaled the end of harvesting and disposal of the remnants of sugar cane plants.

An hour and a half after he had left Katherine at the Royal, Jack arrived at his destination. Haleiwa is a quaint small town situated between two lovely bays of sparkling blue water with art galleries, restaurants, beaches, old houses, and a lot of Hawaiian tradition. Papa David Wai'hee lived in a green wood frame house on a quiet street not far from Waialua Bay. Jack walked up three gray wooden steps to the porch, and Papa David, hearing his footfalls, came to the door.

"Good morning, Mr. Sullivan," he said, emerging from behind the opening screen door.

"Good morning, Papa David."

Papa David was a distinguished looking elderly man of medium height, powerfully built, with short-cropped gray hair.

He wore a brightly colored cotton Aloha shirt outside his beige trousers, and his handshake was firm.

"Thank you for taking the time to see me, Papa David."

"It's no trouble at all. Maile is a great friend of mine. She has helped me wade through the Bishop Museum's collections on many occasions, and I was only too happy to help out a friend of hers. Maile told me you have some questions about Hawaii's poisonous plants. Did you have an unfortunate encounter with one?"

"Sort of, but not directly," Jack replied.

"Did a friend of yours get sick as a result of contact with one of them?"

"Not exactly."

"Let's go inside to get my books, and I'll show you pictures of our botanical neighbors who sometimes look quite beautiful and, therefore, harmless, but nevertheless pack a powerful punch if contacted in the wrong way."

Jack followed Papa David into the living room, where one wall was lined with bookcases. Papa David selected a large book, the size of an atlas, pulled it down from the shelf, and handed it to Jack.

"Would you like some tea, Mr. Sullivan?"

"Please call me Jack and, yes, that would be great."

Papa David went into the kitchen and returned with two cups of tea on a tray. He motioned to Jack to join him on the porch where they sat in rattan rocking chairs facing the bay.

"Do you know what the plant looked like that your friend came into contact with?" asked Papa David.

"That's the problem. We don't know."

"Can you describe the symptoms that your friend manifested after he came into contact with the plant?"

Jack hesitated and looked at Papa David, whose wise eyes persuaded him to share his confidence.

"Papa David, did you read the story in the Advertiser about the Hollywood producer who collapsed at the Diamond Head Canoe Club on Monday night?"

"Yes. Did he have a heart attack as the television news reported?"

"If he did, that wasn't the cause of his death," Jack responded. "He was poisoned. The autopsy revealed a liquid substance in his stomach that had been extracted from a poisonous plant. The police don't know what plant it came from, and the toxicologists are stumped as well."

"And how did you come to learn this, Jack?"

"The police officer in charge of the investigation is a friend of mine and he told me in a sort of quasi-official way so I could help him with one part of the investigation that involves a mutual friend of ours. Not in any criminal sense, of course."

"And you're doing a bit of freelancing, on a quasi-official basis, of course," said Papa David, breaking into a knowing smile.

"I am," Jack conceded.

"Well, the first step in any healing process is to get to know the patient. And if, as I suspect, you are a lawyer, you know that the first step in preparing a witness is also to learn everything you can about him. Correct?" Papa David asked.

"How did you know I'm a lawyer?" Jack asked. "Did Maile tell you?"

"She did, but it would have been obvious in any event, Jack. I rather enjoyed your circumspect approach. It showed your concern for the confidentiality with which you have been entrusted by the police department. We have similar responsibilities in the doctor-patient relationship."

"Thank you, sir," Jack said.

"Now, Jack, tell me about yourself, and then I will tell you who I am and what I do."

Jack told Papa David about Katherine, his family, his education, his service in the Navy, and his work as a lawyer. Upon hearing that Jack's father was also a physician, Papa David launched into a discussion of his own life and his profession.

"Jack, Maile probably told you that I am a 'Kahuna la'au lapa'au', one who is skilled in the art of plant medicine.

'La'au' is the Hawaiian word for plant, 'lapa'au' is Hawaiian for medicine, and you want to know about 'la'au make', which is the Hawaiian way of saying poison. And I'm sure you noticed that the first part of that phrase is the same word that appears in my title – 'la'au', meaning plant. The second word in that phrase, 'make', means death. Literally translated 'la'au make' means plant death, or death by plant. So, you see, we Hawaiians have a long history of dealing with the effects of our people coming into contact with the poisonous plants that abound in these islands."

Jack felt as if he were back in high school, listening to his father explain the Latin and Greek roots of medical terms and other scientific phenomena. Just then, a tall, handsome woman walked out onto the porch. She wore a floor-length pink dress, and her hair was dark brown with streaks of gray. Jack knew instinctively that she was Papa David's wife and stood to greet her.

"Jack, I would like you to meet my wife, Kaiulani."

"It's very nice to meet you, Kaiulani. Your husband is a great teacher."

"That's his way, Jack. It's so nice to meet you as well. May I get you some more tea?"

"No, I'm fine, thank you."

"Then I will leave you two to your discussion. I'm going to visit our daughter down the street."

"Now, where were we, Jack?" Papa David said with a smile.

"You were, like my father, explaining the root meanings of words, in this case the Hawaiian words for poison."

"It's a habit of men of a certain age who were taught the importance of words when they were young," Papa David said.

"Your wife is lovely," Jack told him. "I'm sure any interruption by Kaiulani is a welcome respite from whatever you're doing."

"She's the light of my life. I would be nowhere without her."

"I can feel her effect on you just from the short time she was with us," Jack said.

"We Hawaiians are a very spiritual people, Jack, and we have those kinds of effects on each other, particularly between husband and wife."

"You must meet my wife Katherine. She has the same effect on me."

"Well, Jack, let me tell you more about what I do and perhaps we'll conclude that I can help you. Let me tell you about 'la'au lapa'au'. It is the traditional form of Hawaiian healing. Much of it is spiritual. That's why I wanted to talk to you before we started discussing your question, so that I could understand you and your relationship to the world around you. The medicine that we use is derived from nature. We find it in our backyards and we find it in the mountains and we find it by the sea. I can tell by your smile that you know I'm referring to the plants that grow throughout these islands."

"I knew I came to the right place," Jack said.

"We have learned over time how to use these plants, both alone and in combination with each other, to treat medical conditions."

"Give me an example," Jack asked.

"The bark of a certain shrub can be mixed with the sap of a certain nut to produce a laxative or to cause vomiting."

"Sort of like the green apple quick step," Jack responded with a smile.

"Very similar, Jack. But at the same time, it's important to measure the proportions of fluids extracted from these plants so they don't cause any untoward effects."

"Like poisoning."

"Yes, like all medicines, some of the same plants we use for medicinal purposes can, if administered in too high a dose, be toxic to humans. I have spent my life working with plants and herbs, learning how they affect humans when administered alone and in combination with other plants. It's part of the Hawaiian tradition."

"Maile told me that in Hawaiian tradition, there is a god who held power over poisons," Jack said.

"Ah, Kalaipahoa. He is also called the sorcery god. He's typically portrayed in images made from the wood of three trees that were believed to be poisonous. The Bishop Museum has a wooden statue of Kalaipahoa, and there is a cavity in the back of the statue that was used to hold the poison."

"So poison was used in Hawaiian customs?" Jack asked.

"Yes, in ancient times there were ceremonies where poison was consumed and then followed by taking antidotes, all drawn from parts of plants. The one who consumed the poison would later be saved by consuming the antidote."

"Sounds like a great way to spend an evening," Jack said wryly.

"Well, not exactly, but it was an important element of ancient Hawaiian life. In fact, after the poison had been consumed, the priest would do all kinds of things, some of which were harmful, to heal the person who had consumed the poison."

"Like what?" Jack asked.

"He would consume harmful things."

"Such as?" Jack asked.

"He would drink potions that contained poisons."

"Such as?" Jack asked.

"Oh, there were many different poisons."

"Give me an example."

"Well, one was 'Akia, but there were many others."

"What is 'Akia?"

"Akia is a shrub with oval-shaped green leaves. It has yellow flowers that develop small red berries, and its bark is reddish in color and very hard."

"And it's poisonous?" Jack asked.

"Certain forms of 'Akia are highly poisonous, but, for the most part, they aren't found in the Hawaiian Islands. Only one strain that grows on Oahu is poisonous."

"Just one form of 'Akia found here is poisonous?" Jack asked.

"Yes, but there are many other very poisonous plants on this island. For example, the Be-Still tree grows in many backyards and it contains a substance that is very toxic, particularly to the heart."

"How does it work?"

"It contains cardiac glycosides that block electrical impulses throughout the body by interfering with the exchange of sodium and potassium in and out of the nerve and muscle cells. All parts of this tree are extremely dangerous."

"And they're everywhere?"

"Everywhere."

"What else is poisonous?"

"Oleander bushes, which grow in yards and parks and along roads all over the islands."

"How dangerous is Oleander?"

"All parts of the Oleander bush contain cardiac glycosides that interfere with the heart, just like the Be-Still tree."

"Any others?"

"Jimsonweed is extremely toxic. It contains chemicals that affect the central nervous system. Black-eyed Susans contain tox-albumins that interfere with the functioning of the cells in the liver, kidneys and nerves."

"Papa David, how many of these plants are there in Hawaii?" Jack asked.

"Jack, there are many, and books have been written about them. Their properties are well-known by physicians."

"If that's the case, why can't the State's toxicologists identify the source of the fluid in Reynolds' stomach?" Jack inquired.

"There are some plants that are seen often, and others that may not be seen in a lifetime," Papa David responded.

"So the plants growing in backyards and parks and along roads are more likely to be consumed than ones that are not so prevalent?"

"Exactly."

"And if the fluid in Reynolds' system came from one of the latter category of plants, it's possible that no toxicologist alive today has ever seen it before."

"Correct, but they should be able to identify its chemical components. That would give us some idea of the kind of plant they came from," Papa David explained.

"Of course, but that would only identify the chemical reaction that caused the death. It wouldn't necessarily identify the plant because, as you pointed out, some plants cause harm by the same means, for example, by interfering with the heart's electrical impulses."

"Yes, counselor. You must be very effective when cross-examining expert witnesses. I enjoy your analysis, Jack. Very few people take the time to think things through these days."

"I think I need to do a little more reading and thinking about the facts of this case," Jack said.

"There are many books at the Bishop Museum that can help you. Please come back if I can be of any further assistance."

"I will. And thank you very much for your time and your wisdom, Papa David,"

"You're welcome, Jack, and I'll look forward to our next visit."

"Me, too," Jack said, shaking Papa David's hand.

CHAPTER SEVENTEEN

Jack decided to return to Waikiki the long way, driving north along Kamehameha Highway, past the famous North Shore surfing beaches at Waimea Bay, the Banzai Pipeline, and Sunset Beach. During the winter months, these beaches confront Pacific swells that start to build thousands of miles away, sometimes off the coast of Alaska. They march unimpeded across the Pacific, increasing in height and strength until they break as monstrous waves on the reefs that protect the northern coast of Oahu. These are the most famous surfing beaches in the world and they gave rise to the unique culture and language that marks surfers around the world.

When Jack reached Kahuku Point at the northern tip of Oahu, he followed the highway as it turned south past Turtle Bay and the ruins of sugar mills and drove toward Laie Bay, made famous by the traditional Hawaiian song called the Hukilau. The ultramarine Pacific sparkled and seemed to flow into the azure sky at the horizon, making Jack feel as if he were inside a blue silk tent whose sides and top were billowing in the wind.

Reflecting on what he had learned from Papa David, Jack concluded that he had to do more research at the Bishop Museum. He remained puzzled at the inability of toxicologists to identify the source of the fluid that had poisoned Derek Reynolds. These plants have been poisoning people in Hawaii for a long time, and medical doctors as well as herbal medicine practitioners were familiar with their properties. Why couldn't they identify this particular plant?

Jack passed the island that looks like and takes its name from a Chinaman's Hat and saw a military jet landing at the Marine Corps Air Station at Kaneohe Bay in the distance. As he approached the peninsula where the base is situated, Jack realized he was passing the place where Kulani had been run off the road near Lanikai. The road ran right next to the beach, and it was clear that one car could easily push another off the road and onto the sand.

He drove along the beach road for a while and then cut over to Kalanianaole Highway, which meanders along the southeast coast of Oahu, known as the Windward Shore because the prevailing tradewinds blow toward that side of the island. Rounding Makapuu Point, Jack headed west toward Waikiki and marveled at the green-covered volcanic mountains, lush with vegetation, that spilled down to the sparkling blue sea a thousand feet below. Like a mirage, they presented an image that no camera lens could capture. Looking at the expanse of green on his right, Jack realized that he had a daunting task ahead of him — trying to identify one plant among the thousands that covered this island.

It was close to five o'clock when he turned into the driveway of the Royal Hawaiian and walked over to Katherine's dress shop.

"Hellooo," he said as he opened the door to the light ring of the bell.

Katherine responded with a big smile as she walked quickly toward him. They embraced and kissed, observing their silent moment together at the end of the day, and held each other tightly, not wanting to let go.

"Did any more nice Japanese ladies come by?" Jack asked.

"No, but a very nice young German lady did and she bought two of my dresses and one evening sarong."

"Wonderful," Jack said, "you'll soon be known as the designer to the Axis Powers."

"Now, Jack, you know we own a Mercedes and we used to have a Lexus."

"True, true. You know my father still won't buy a Japanese car," Jack said.

"I know, but he has a Mercedes. How does he justify that?" Katherine asked.

"I asked him that question once," Jack replied.

"And what was his rationale for the distinction?" Katherine asked. "Germany and Japan were both enemies of the United States in World War II."

"It's the sneak attack. That's how he distinguishes between the Germans and the Japanese and rationalizes the Mercedes but not a Lexus."

"Your father is something else."

"Well, he was a Naval Officer in World War II. As far as I'm concerned, he's entitled to his views. He earned them the hard way."

"That's for sure," Katherine said.

"What do you say we close this place and go for a swim. I've got a lot to tell you."

"I've got a lot to tell you too, Jack. Hypatia and Jennifer were in today. We had a long talk about all kinds of things."

Jack and Katherine walked back to the Royal Hawaiian, changed into their bathing suits, and headed for the beach. Nearly all of the tourists had returned to their rooms, leaving much of the most famous beach in the world to Jack and Katherine. As they waded into the Pacific, Jack held Katherine's hand and guided her around the coral heads that occasionally surfaced above the sand at their feet. They swam out fifty yards and floated on their backs. Then Jack stood up and put his arms around Katherine's waist, allowing her to wrap her legs around his waist, lean back and float on her back while they talked. Jack told her all about Papa David and the poisonous plants that live sometimes in harmony and sometimes in conflict with the people of Hawaii.

"We've probably stood next to those plants hundreds of times," Katherine said.

"No doubt about it. It was a surprise to me. I had no idea so many plants that you see every day can kill you."

"I'll have to be more careful the next time I pick out plants for my shop."

"For the most part, it seems you have to eat them to cause any real damage," Jack said.

"Well, I'm not taking any chances. In fact, I'm going to talk to Jennifer about it."

"What does Jennifer know about Hawaiian plants?" Jack asked.

"Quite a bit, Jack. She owns a flower shop in Beverly Hills and comes here all the time to see a florist who supplies her with tropical flowers."

"So Hypatia and Jennifer came by to visit you?"

"They came in about ten-thirty, and we had coffee and talked about Derek, the movie, and fashion."

"Did they seem upset?"

"Not particularly, although Hypatia is concerned that progress on the movie will slow down. I think she wants to get this whole thing over with and go home."

"I'll bet she's relieved that she won't have to deal with Reynolds anymore."

"She seemed to be. In fact, she told me that she had dinner with Commander Butler last night. They're old sweethearts, and she was just thrilled to run into him at the Club. I think the spark we saw on Monday night has turned into a flame."

"How did Jennifer seem?"

"She was quiet, but what little sister wouldn't be in the presence of a star like Hypatia. People walked into the shop and just gawked when they saw who was in there."

"How did Jennifer get into the flower business?"

"Well, that's interesting. I was talking to Hypatia about a dress she liked, which had a tropical floral pattern, and Jennifer knew the name of every flower on the dress. She was also looking at the flowers and plants that I have around the shop that, I hope, are not poisonous and she told me that she owns a flower shop in Beverly Hills. She and Hypatia are partners in the business. Hypatia supplied the money to get the business going, and Jennifer manages it. They not only sell flowers and plants to the stars; they also supply them for movie and television sets. It's quite a business."

"And Jennifer comes over here regularly?" Jack asked.

"Yes, she buys tropical flowers and plants from a wholesale florist here on Oahu who ships them to her in California."

"Who would that be?"

"I don't know. I didn't ask, but she said she'd have him send some plants to my shop."

"Be sure to find out what they are before you touch them, Katherine."

"I will, you old worry wart."

"And do me a favor, will you? Save the invoice when they're delivered."

"Do you want to buy some tropical plants for our house on the Big Island?"

"No. I think the Kailua Plantation staff has that covered. I'd just like to know who her supplier is."

"Okay. Now, Jack, it's date night and while we usually go out for dinner on date night, I have a proposal for you."

"What are you thinking?"

"I think we should have a naked date night at home."

"You're on. Let's get out of here," Jack said with a broad grin as he led her swimming in strong strokes toward the beach.

CHAPTER EIGHTEEN

Jack woke up at seven on Friday morning to the low, steady breathing of his wife. Her blonde hair cascaded over the side of the pillow, and she gave no sign of getting up anytime soon. But as he swung his legs out of the bed, Katherine reached over and touched his back.

"Where are you going, wild man?"

"And I thought you were sound asleep."

"I was, until you got up," she replied coyly, her voice deep and raspy with invitation.

"I don't really feel like getting up," Jack said with a grin.

"Neither do I, handsome. Come back here."

The telephone in their bedroom rang at eight, and Katherine handed Jack the receiver.

"Hello, Jack. This is Peter Dillingham."

"Good morning, Peter, and to what do I owe such an early greeting from the distinguished manager of Hawaii's most famous hotel?"

"Jack, I'm sorry to call you this early but I have great news and I wanted to let you and Katherine know as soon as possible. The radio show is all set. We go on the air Monday afternoon, broadcasting and streaming from the Mai Tai Bar, and I wanted to make sure that you and Katherine could be there. I've reserved two seats at my table for you and I've also asked Arthur Fairbanks and the Grant's to sit with us."

"Wonderful, Peter, we can't wait. What time should we arrive?"

"To accommodate listeners on the east coast, the show starts at four o'clock, so it would be best to be in your seats by three-thirty."

"We'll be there, Peter. Thanks for calling."

"He certainly is excited about the radio show," Jack said to Katherine after he hung up.

"I know. Georgia told me Peter consulted her about it, because she remembers the old show at the Moana Surfrider so well."

"Did Georgia ever sing on the show?"

"Yes, she did. Of course, she was a very young girl then, but it was a popular show that was broadcast all over the world."

"It must have been thrilling to sit on the east coast during a cold winter night, next to an old Zenith or Silvertone radio, and listen to music from Hawaii, when the only way to get there was by cruise ship from the west coast."

"That's how my grandparents traveled to Hawaii. They sailed on the *Lurline*, which was a very elegant ocean liner. Dinner was black tie every night, and the menus were hand-painted and engraved."

Jack shook his head. "What a great way to get here."

"And it took nearly a week from San Francisco! By the time they arrived and spent another two or three weeks, I'm amazed they could ever come home."

"And therein, lovely one, lies the reason that we, too, are here," Jack said with a smile.

"You're right, Jack; at least we come by it honestly."

"That we do, my dear. And here's to Peter for bringing Old Hawaii back. People seem to be searching for traditional things, and this show will be just like the one their parents and grandparents enjoyed years ago. I'll bet Georgia will sing in the show."

"I have no doubt. I just hope the cloud of this Derek Reynolds thing isn't still hanging over Gordon by then."

"Me too," Jack said. "And I'll do my part to remove that cloud today. I'm going back to the Bishop Museum and try to find out what plant was the source of the fluid that killed Reynolds."

"Don't you think you should leave that to the police, Jack?"

"I'm not interfering with their investigation. I'm just augmenting it with my own research. They're short on resources, and I'm helping out."

"Okay, Detective, but don't get so far into it that the murderer gets wind of it and comes after you."

"I won't," Jack said as he kissed Katherine's forehead. "In fact, I'll check in with the Plantation by phone this morning and then I'll call those chefs in New York and Washington who think espresso is the only kind of coffee you should serve in good restaurants."

"Remember, someone ran Kulani off the road."

"Don't worry. I'll be careful."

"Please be extremely careful," Katherine said as she looked at their clock radio and realized it was later than she thought.

"Oh Jack, I'm really late. I've got to take the first shower this morning."

Jack made coffee and popped whole wheat bread into the toaster, then cut up papaya and mango, which he doused with the juice of a freshly squeezed lime. He took the fruit out to the lanai and sat down to watch the morning rituals of the surfers, beach boys and catamaran skippers. He never tired of observing these daily rites and liked to think that, from his post in the tower, he participated in their routines.

Katherine joined him on the lanai and smiled when she saw toast alongside the slices of mango and papaya.

"What time are you going to the Bishop Museum?"

"Right after I finish making my calls to Keoni and the east coast."

"Jack, I'm really looking forward to dinner at the Club tonight with the Grant's."

"So am I."

Katherine stood up and Jack pulled her to him. They embraced and kissed, and Katherine left for the Halekulani. Then Jack walked into the kitchen and called Keoni Campbell at the Plantation.

"Good morning, Keoni. How are things on the Big Island?"

"Everything's in order. We're roasting this morning, and the tourist trade has picked up."

"At the Plantation or on the internet?" Jack asked.

"Both. I'm going to start asking visitors how they learned about us."

"That would be a useful piece of information. Maybe we should beef up our website."

"Let's see what kind of feedback I get."

"Good idea, Keoni. I'm going to call those damn chefs and restaurant managers on the east coast this morning and try to persuade them to move into the 21st Century."

"I don't envy you, Mr. Sullivan."

"No, dialing for dollars has never been a favorite pastime of mine."

After calling twenty restaurants in New York and ten in Washington, Jack decided he'd had enough of that for the day. He was not comfortable asking people to buy his coffee, even though he believed it was the best in the islands. He headed downstairs to the elevator, looking forward to another day of botanical research at the Bishop Museum. As the elevator doors opened on the lobby, Jack saw Arthur Fairbanks striding in from the courtyard.

"Arthur, good morning."

"Good morning, Jack. And how do you do?" Arthur inquired with a slight bow and tilt of his lightly feathered crown.

"I'm fine. I understand from talking with Peter that we'll be sitting together at the opening of his radio show."

"Indeed. Did he ring you, as he did me, early this morning?"

"He did. He's very excited about it."

"Quite. And I must say that I am as well. It will restore a charming part of Hawaii's past. Now Jack, have you heard anything more about Derek Reynolds?"

"Not much, Arthur. I assume the police are conducting their investigation."

"Yes, they rang me yesterday. Interrupted me just as I was about to dial my bootmaker in London. They're interviewing everyone who was at the party. Strange, they asked me quite a bit about the Lane's. Have you been interviewed?"

"No, but I'm sure I'll get a call."

"A sad event and such a bother for the Club," Arthur said.

"Yes," Jack responded. "Speaking of the Lane's, Arthur, how well did they know Derek?"

"Extremely well. As I said the other night, they were colleagues in Hollywood until Derek chose another actress for the lead role that should have been Sidney's. Why do you ask?"

"Well, I had dinner at the Poinciana on Tuesday night with Stanton Char, and we got talking to the maitre'd. Stanton knows him. He told us that Reynolds caused quite a ruckus in the dining room last Saturday night when he was having dinner with Hypatia and her sister Jennifer. That must be the scene you told me about on Monday night at the cast party."

"Yes, no doubt, but what possible connection does that have to the Lane's?" Arthur asked.

"They were in the restaurant when it happened. They must have seen and heard it, but they just got up and left the dining room without so much as acknowledging Derek's presence."

"Maybe they didn't want to embarrass him," Arthur observed.

"Maybe, but they also unexpectedly checked out the next morning."

"They probably couldn't stand the thought of being in the same hotel with Reynolds. Given their history with him, I can't say that I blame them."

"Where do the Lane's live here on Oahu?"

"They have a spectacular place out at Lanikai on the Windward Shore."

"Big?" Jack asked.

"Quite, and it's marvelously landscaped with every imaginable type of tropical plant and flower. Sidney and George fell madly in love with Hawaii when they moved here and set out to learn everything they could about Hawaiian customs and traditions. Their house and gardens are modeled after those of Hawaiian royalty. You really should pop over and see it. I'll mention it to them. I'm sure they'd be pleased to show it to you. Well, I shall look forward to seeing you at Dillingham's show on Monday afternoon. God Save the Queen!" Arthur proclaimed before marching off through the lobby.

As Jack stood in the Royal Hawaiian's driveway waiting for his Jeep, he realized that today's research could be very important.

CHAPTER NINETEEN

By leaving Waikiki at ten-thirty in the morning, Jack avoided both the rush hour traffic on H-1, and the late morning lunch crowd heading to Waikiki's hotels for a surfside noon meal. Maile smiled as Jack entered the library stacks and waved at him.

"I heard your meeting with Papa David went well. He was very impressed with your preparation."

"You talked to him?"

"Yes, he called this morning to tell me how much he enjoyed meeting you and to suggest some books you may want to take a look at."

"What a guy. He's very thoughtful."

"That's his line of work, Jack, helping people."

"I'll have to call and thank him."

"You can tell him the next time you see him. He's sure you'll be by again soon."

"He's probably right about that."

Maile gave Jack a list of several books that Papa David had asked her to pass on to Jack. Jack took the list and walked to the stacks. The books fell into two categories: medical references and Hawaiian customs and traditions. The medical books identified poisonous plants and ways to treat people who had come into contact with them. Jack decided to start with them.

Unlike the treatises he had examined on his previous visit to the museum, these references featured enlarged color photographs of the plants. Jack was struck by the range and beauty of plants that were toxic enough to kill a man.

When he saw a large color photograph of the Be-Still Tree, he recognized its yellow flowers immediately; he had seen them on the lanai outside Stanton Char's house. He also recognized the enlarged photograph of Oleander, which lined the driveway of another friend's house on Oahu, creating a very private and, he now knew, very dangerous path to the front door.

Jack realized that he had also seen the Angel's Trumpet, an attractive tree with cream and yellow-colored trumpet-shaped flowers that hang upside down, all over Oahu. And he recognized its relative, the Jimsonweed, by its thorny apple-like berry. In fact, as he looked at each photograph, Jack realized that he had frequently been in close company with many of Hawaii's poisonous plants but hadn't known they were so dangerous.

The medical literature confirmed Papa David's description of the effects these poisonous plants have on humans who consume them, but went further. These books also contained detailed descriptions of the symptoms that would be evident in someone who had consumed one of the plants and recommendations for appropriate medical treatment.

Jack then turned to the other references that Papa David had provided, the ones that described the roles plants played in Hawaiian customs and traditions. He thought it just might be possible that the plant that did Derek Reynolds in was rare enough that it might not be seen by toxicologists in a lifetime, but might be one that had been used in ancient Hawaiian ceremonies. If so, it could have been discovered by someone who researched the use of plants in Hawaiian customs.

He found a wealth of information about the use of plants in Hawaiian traditions and rituals. In one custom, a statue of Kalaipahoa, which Papa David said had been carved out of poisonous woods, was used in an elaborate ceremony of near death and recovery. Cups of kava, a pepper root drink, would be prepared for the 'kahu' or priests, and one of the 'kahu' would scrape poisonous wood from the Kalaipahoa statue into one cup of kava and drink from that cup while the other 'kahu' drank from cups that contained only kava. The 'kahu' who had consumed the kava with scrapings from what was regarded as the body of Kalaipahoa would then pray for the life of the king, the chiefs, and the people as he began to gasp and turn red. At that point, the other 'kahu' would give him an antidote to the poison by applying a bark that was regarded as a healing substance to his lips, and the poisoned 'kahu' would recover.

But the remedies used by sorcerers really caught Jack's attention. One skilled in the art of sorcery or black magic was known as a 'kahu 'ana 'ana' or as a 'kahuna 'ana 'ana'. They used prayer as their primary method of treating illness that had been caused by the sorcery of another. First, they said a prayer to drive sickness from the patient by removing the evil influence that had been visited on the patient by the sorcerer. When the prayers for release were as powerful as the wrongdoer's prayer for harm, the evil influence would be eliminated. A secondary treatment was known as 'hai haia'. Here, the 'kahuna 'ana 'ana' would try to cure his patient by acting insane in an effort to prevent the gods from hearing the rival's curses, drawing the curses to himself, and thus freeing the victim. Then, with his superior 'mana' or spirit, the 'kahuna' would drive the curses away and direct them at the rival sorcerer. One way that the 'kahuna' would act insane was to drink potions that contained poisons, such as 'Auhuhu, a slender legume used to poison fish; Ipu Awa Awa, a gourd whose pulp was used as medicine; 'Opihi Awa, a nonedible limpet used in sorcery; Kumimi, an inedible crab used in sorcery; and 'Akia, a shrub whose bark, roots and leaves were used to poison fish.

Jack's interest was immediately piqued by the potions that contained 'Akia, the poisonous plant Papa David had said was rare but nevertheless found on Oahu, particularly because 'Akia was the only source of poison listed that was a shrub whose bark was poisonous. Dr. Wong had been clear about the poison that killed Derek Reynolds: It had been extracted from a shrub that had bark on it.

Jack knew he had to learn more about 'Akia. His eyes raced down the list of books that Papa David had recommended and focused on one that explained the roles that plants played in the ancient rituals of Hawaii. He searched for 'Akia and found it in the middle of the book. Four words on the first page of its description leapt out at him, "extremely poisonous if eaten."

The text echoed Papa David's words. It described 'Akia as a shrub with many branches and green oval-shaped leaves. Its yellow flowers develop red fruits or berries not quite half an inch in diameter, and its bark is extremely strong. In fact, because of the strength of its bark, Hawaiians had used it as a binding material. But the description of this member of the Wikstroemia genus was secondary to the warning about its toxicity. Although harmless to the touch, 'Akia was extremely poisonous if eaten.

Indeed, it had been used by ancient Hawaiians in a potion concocted for two purposes: suicide and the execution of criminals upon the order of a chief. For the latter purpose, the ritual, like all others, was prescribed with particularity. The doomed man would be presented with the poison in a cup and then toasted by the executioner with the sarcastic expression, "He wahi mea ola ia", which literally means "This is to keep you alive." Today, Jack thought, the executioner would probably say "To your health and prosperity."

Jack read further and learned that the fluid in 'Akia affects the central nervous system and that Hawaiians had also used it to catch fish. They would place it among stones at the bottom of a tidal pool and wait for ten minutes. The fish would then appear near the surface, swimming aimlessly in a drugged state until they died. As with the symptoms manifested by Derek Reynolds just before he collapsed, there was no violent seizure evident in the fish that had consumed 'Akia.

Now he needed to find out where 'Akia grew. Turning to another reference book that listed every plant in the islands, he found its botanical name. More than twenty species of 'Akia could be found in the Hawaiian Islands. Just as Papa David had told him, with the exception of one species on Oahu, they were either harmless or only mildly toxic.

Jack now set out to find the toxic species of Wikstroemia Oahuensis. He knew that Papa David was his best shot at finding where on Oahu this poisonous plant grew.

CHAPTER TWENTY

Jack called Papa David from Maile's desk and asked if he could drop by for another visit. When Papa David said he had the afternoon free, Jack was ecstatic. Maile smiled and wished him good luck as he hurried out of the stacks.

The sugar cane fields were a blur of green and red as the blue Jeep sped along the highway. Jack was riveted on his discovery of 'Akia's use in Hawaiian traditions and its glaring absence from lists of the most common poisonous plants in Hawaii. As he passed Schofield Barracks on his left, his cell phone rang. It was Katherine.

"I've got some news for you," she said. "The flowers and plants that Jennifer said she would send from her wholesaler just arrived, and I have the florist's name. It's called Tropical Flora. Do you want the phone number?"

"No, just tell me where it is."

"It's in Kailua on Kailua Road right in the center of town."

Katherine gave Jack the address and then hung up to talk to a customer who had just walked into the shop. As Jack put his cell phone down, he had a premonition that he would find 'Akia on the Windward Shore of Oahu, not far from either Kailua or Lanikai.

Less than an hour after he left the Bishop Museum, Jack was bounding up the porch steps of Papa David's house. The elderly man met him at the door with a smile.

"You're a quick study, Jack."

"Let's just say I got lucky, because I can't say that I've mastered the subject matter yet. But I do have enough to act on, at least preliminarily."

"Come in and tell me what you've found."

Jack told Papa David about the Hawaiian ceremony that incorporated 'Akia in the potion given to condemned criminals and the accompanying sarcastic toast to the condemned man's future well-being.

"Yes, that is an old custom," Papa David said. "And 'Akia would have been the constituent that caused the criminal's death. But why do you think that's relevant to your case?"

"Because the toxicologists would have been familiar with all the other commonly encountered poisonous plants and would have recognized their properties immediately. This is one plant they rarely see and, as far as I can tell, it's the only plant with poisonous bark that was used to make those potions the kahu's drank. Plus this one had a certain irony in the way it was administered to criminals."

"You mean whoever put this in Derek Reynolds' Mai Tai, would have enjoyed seeing him toasted before he drank it?"

"Precisely."

"Well, Jack, your theory has a certain diabolical logic."

"That's what I think. Plus you can find it if you do the research."

"Where would you like to go from here?"

"I'd like to go to wherever it is on Oahu that the one strain of poisonous 'Akia grows."

"That's easy enough. I know it well. I've seen the virulent form of 'Akia in only one place on Oahu – a field just above Kailua."

Bingo, Jack thought. "Can we go there now?"

"Certainly, but let me get some gloves and a pair of shears. I'm sure you'll want to take a sample back with you."

"Papa David, you're one step ahead of me."

"Just barely, Jack. Let's call it a half step."

Jack helped Papa David climb into the Jeep, and they drove north and then east from the North Shore of Oahu to its Windward Shore. When they arrived at the town of Kailua an hour later, Papa David directed Jack to turn off King Kamehameha Highway and drive west on the road that led to the hills above Kailua. When they reached a field, Papa David told Jack to stop. They got out of the Jeep, and he led Jack across the small plain toward a line of low-lying light green shrubs that grew together, close to the ground, at the back of the field.

"Jack, this is 'Akia."

"It looks just like the photo I saw. It's hard to believe it's dangerous."

"Hold this branch so I can cut it. It's harmless to touch but wash your hands before you eat and don't touch your mouth or your eyes after you touch this bush."

Papa David took the shears in his gloved right hand and reached into the bush. With some difficulty, he cut a long branch with several pairs of leaves and pulled it free of the shrub.

"Is that enough for analysis?" Jack asked.

"Yes, but if we need more, these bushes aren't going anywhere."

Jack held the branch in front of him and examined the green leaves, red berries, and reddish bark. He studiously avoided breaking the skin on the berries or cracking the bark. But as he turned to walk back toward the Jeep, Jack noticed a white spot on the ground beneath one of the bushes, several feet from the branch that Papa David had cut, and pointed it out to him.

Papa David crawled under the bush and examined the small white object that looked, at first, like a piece of coral.

"Jack, I think we've just found evidence of prior human interest in 'Akia."

"What is it?"

"A cigarette butt."

"Let me take a look at it," Jack said as he crawled under the bush.

"A Camel. Must be a tough guy. Or gal."

Jack looked deeper into the shrub, above the cigarette butt, and noticed that several branches appeared to be arranged in an unnatural fashion. Peering into the shrub, Jack found what he was looking for – the stub of a branch that had recently been cut close to the bottom of the bush.

"Papa David, this branch was cut with a very sharp blade. As hard as this bark is, it's not broken or shredded. Someone came in here with a tool that could cut through very hard things, someone who must have known how hard the bark of 'Akia is."

Papa David leaned forward to look for himself.

"You're right, Jack. This is a clean cut that took off a large branch."

"Let's have a look around and see if we can find anything else."

They walked around the field near the 'Akia shrubs but found nothing. As Papa David surveyed the other plants that grew near the 'Akia, Jack walked toward the road. On the edge of the road, where it met the mud on the field, he found what he was looking for.

"I've found tire tread marks in the mud. It's just where you would stop if you had pulled a little off the road but didn't want to drive onto the field near the shrub."

"You're right. There's just enough room on the left side for another car to get by."

"Just enough room to avoid attracting a passerby's attention," Jack added. "I've got a digital camera in the glove compartment and I'm going to take some pictures of that bush, the cigarette butt, and these tire marks before we leave."

After photographing what they had found, Jack grabbed a piece of paper from the Jeep and walked back to the bush. He used the paper to lift the cigarette butt from the ground without touching it and wrapped the paper around it.

"I have to admit I'm getting a kick out of this," he said.

"I can tell."

The sun was low on the horizon when Jack dropped Papa David off at his house in Haleiwa.

"Thank you for helping me this afternoon, Papa David."

"It was my pleasure, Jack. Let me know if I can help in any other way."

"You've already been more than helpful. I can't thank you enough, and I'll keep you posted."

Jack called Katherine on his cell phone.

"Good news. I think I made a breakthrough in the case today. I've got to see Dave as soon as possible. Do you mind my being a little late getting home tonight?"

"Not at all, I have some paperwork to do anyway. I'll keep my cell phone on wherever I am. But remember, we've got reservations at the Club for dinner with the Grants at eight-thirty."

"I'll be home by eight."

Jack immediately dialed Dave McNeil's number at Police Headquarters.

"Dave."

"Jack, I wondered when I'd hear from you."

"I've got something. Can I meet you at your office?"

"Come on down. Shall I call Dr. Wong?"

"Yes."

CHAPTER TWENTY ONE

The sugar cane and pineapple fields that lined Kamehameha Highway whizzed by as Jack sped south from Haleiwa toward H-2 and their green crops took on a neon glow as they reflected the red tones of the setting sun. By the time he reached H-2, the sun had set and Jack turned the Jeep's headlights on. They revealed a plain on either side of the highway, dense with sugar cane and pineapples.

At Pearl City, Jack bore left onto H-1 and headed toward downtown Honolulu. He was convinced he had found evidence that would lead him and the police to the person who had poisoned Derek Reynolds.

Holding the branch of 'Akia in his left hand, Jack strode into Dave McNeil's office, where Dave and Dr. Wong were sitting, drinking coffee.

"Have you been trimming hedges at the Royal Hawaiian, Jack?" Dave asked with a broad grin.

"No, but I have been cutting shrubs out on the Windward Shore near Kailua and this bud's for you."

"What is it?"

Dr. Wong immediately recognized it. "It's 'Akia, Dave, a very common ornamental shrub found everywhere on the island."

"That's right, Doctor, but this particular 'Akia is not like the 'Akia found in other places on Oahu," Jack explained. "This one is extremely toxic if consumed by humans."

"And how do you know that?" Dr. Wong asked.

"I've been doing research at the Bishop Museum, and I've been talking with Papa David Wai'hee, who took me to the field near Kailua where this one grows."

"Papa David is a very well-respected practitioner of herbal medicine, Dave," Dr. Wong told the detective.

"Yes, he is, and he confirmed the research I did at the Museum," Jack went on. "This particular form of 'Akia is poisonous and it was used in an ancient Hawaiian ceremony to execute criminals by having them drink a potion with 'Akia mixed in."

"This is a new one for me, Dave," Dr. Wong said. "I'm familiar with most of the poisonous plants on the island but I didn't know that 'Akia was poisonous."

"Don't feel bad, Doctor. There's only one kind that's poisonous and, according to Papa David, it only grows in one place on all of Oahu."

"Thank God for small favors," Dave added.

"So I assume you want me to extract fluid from this branch and compare it with the fluid from Derek Reynolds' stomach to see if we get a match," Dr. Wong said to Jack.

"I do, and I'm willing to bet that you'll get one."

"How much, Jack. A cigar from your private stock? A pound of your best Kailua Plantation coffee?" Dave asked with a smile.

"Your choice, Dave, for another round of golf at your club."

"I'll take it to the lab first thing in the morning, and we should have the results back by noon tomorrow," Dr. Wong added.

"Excellent, but that's not all I have for you," Jack said.

"You've been busy," Dave observed.

"Yes, I have." Jack pulled the paper containing the Camel cigarette butt out of his pocket and placed it and his digital camera on the detective's desk.

"The 'Akia bush I found out there had been cut by a very sharp tool, probably very recently, and the other branches of the bush had been rearranged to hide the cut. I've got pictures that show it. And I found this cigarette butt on the ground under the branch that had been cut."

Dave took the cigarette butt from Jack's paper with a pair of tweezers that he drew from his desk drawer and placed it in a plastic evidence bag.

"I hope you didn't touch this butt with your hands. We might be able to get some evidence from it," Dave said.

"I know how to play the game, Dave. But, at a minimum, we now know that the person who left it smokes Camels and is interested in 'Akia."

"We may very well be able to get even more useful evidence from it," Dave said.

"Like DNA?" Jack asked.

"Yes, and maybe even a fingerprint."

"I've got more," Jack announced, pointing to his digital camera on Dave's desk. "Photographs of tire tracks on the edge of the field. Someone had pulled off the road just far enough to let a car pass by."

Jack pushed his digital camera across the desk to Dave and asked him to display the photographs on his computer.

"These are great pictures, Jack. They're very clear," Dave said.

"They're yours, old boy. Just maintain the chain of custody on all this stuff, and we'll have the beginnings of a case with some very tangible as well as demonstrative evidence."

"Spoken like a true prosecutor. I appreciate you efforts, Jack, and I'll let you know what the lab says."

"Thanks, Dave. And, by the way, I'm having dinner with Gordon tonight. Do you want me to pass anything on to him?"

"Just tell him we're hoping to wrap the interviews up in a day or so."

"I'll do it. Have a good evening, Dr. Wong."

Jack was elated as he got back into his Jeep and drove to the Royal Hawaiian. He was confident he had discovered evidence of a crime and not merely the remnants of a botanical field trip. His exuberance was apparent when he opened the door to their apartment and saw Katherine smiling at him.

"You've obviously solved the mystery of Derek Reynolds' murder," Katherine said.

"How can you tell?"

"It's written all over your face. Jump in the shower and get dressed. We're running late. You can tell me all about it on the way to the Club."

By the time they reached the Diamond Head Canoe Club, Jack had recited the entire chronology of his day: learning of the Lanes' interest in Hawaiian plants; reading about the use of 'Akia in ancient Hawaiian rituals; finding the poisonous 'Akia shrubs that had recently been cut, the cigarette butt, and the tire tracks in the field near Kailua; and finally, his meeting with Dave McNeil and Dr. Wong.

"I think you're on the right track, Jack. It certainly feels that way."

"That's what I think. Now I've got to take the next step."

"What's that?"

"I'll tell you after dinner," Jack said as they entered the Club and greeted Noa Watson.

While Katherine stopped to talk to Noa, Jack noticed Sidney Lane sitting alone at the bar and waved to her.

"Jack," Sidney said, waving back at him and motioning for him to join her.

"Hello, Sidney, how are you?"

"I'm fine, Jack. And you?"

"I'm well. Is George here?"

"Yes, somewhere. Jack, I ran into Arthur Fairbanks today, and he mentioned your interest in Hawaiian plants. How have you developed an interest in such an arcane part of Hawaii's culture?"

"Oh, I'm trying to learn as much as I can about Hawaii now that we're living here."

"We did the same thing when we first came here."

"Yes, Arthur told me you have quite a garden. I'd love to see it."

"George and I would be thrilled to have you come by. Just give us a call. We love to show off our gardens."

"Thank you, Sidney. I'll do that."

"Say hello to Katherine for me."

"I will."

Katherine had made her way to the Grants' table out on the Lanai next to the seawall. As President of the Club, Gordon had exclusive use of the President's Table, which had the best view of Waikiki and, behind it, the City of Honolulu. The President's table also enjoyed the delightful accompaniment of the Pacific surf as it danced against the seawall that separated the Lanai from the ocean.

"Sullivan, you didn't paddle today," Gordon called as Jack approached.

"How do you know that?"

"I know all. I have sources. The waves tell me. The fish tell me. The birds tell me."

"You're right. I was doing some research."

"Research is no excuse, Sullivan. You must serve the master of the seas or be forever barred from Neptune's Kingdom."

"Jack, ignore my husband. He's full of himself as usual. How are you, my dear?" Georgia said as Jack sat down at the table.

"I'm well. And you?"

"Wonderful. I'm here with my best friend, your beautiful and glamorous wife."

"You are too much," Katherine said.

"By the way, Jack, I saw you talking to Sidney Lane at the bar. What was that about?"

"Oh, I've developed an interest in tropical plants and I mentioned it to Arthur Fairbanks, who told me about the Lanes' gardens out on the Windward Shore. Arthur told Sidney of my interest, and she invited me to stop by for a tour."

"They're spectacular," Gordon observed.

"I agree," Georgia said. "Gordon and I have been out there several times. She and George know everything about tropical plants and even how they were used in Hawaiian ceremonies."

"Well, I told her I'd stop by soon and have a look."

"Is Sidney alone, Jack?" Georgia asked.

"No, I think George is here. Why?"

"Oh, I thought she might be meeting that young actor I talked to at the party Monday night," Georgia said with a conspiratorial wink.

"You mean Lance Forbes? Why in the world would Sidney be meeting him here?" Katherine asked.

"Well, I saw him hitting on her Monday night. He really does have a thing for older actresses."

"Georgia, just because he was talking to her doesn't mean he was hitting on her," Gordon chided.

"I know what I'm talking about. He talked to her for quite a while after he talked to me. Trust me. They had moved beyond the weather and the waves."

"Well, there's George heading into the bar, so I guess that mystery is solved," Gordon said. "No scandal tonight, my dear. Now let's order before the kitchen closes."

After they ordered, Jack and Gordon discussed the interviews that Dave McNeil was overseeing.

"Jack, the detectives have been interviewing employees here at the Club."

"Anything turn up yet?"

"Not that they've told me."

"That's not unusual, Gordon. They usually keep that stuff to themselves."

"Well, on a lighter note, are you and Katherine ready for Dillingham's radio show?"

"We are. Peter's been so enthusiastic that I thought he was about to require black tie for the inaugural broadcast."

"He really should," Katherine observed.

"That would be elegant, but no one in Hawaii dresses for dinner these days," Georgia said.

"I'll wear my finest silk Aloha shirt," Gordon said with authority.

"You know, he's put us all at the table closest to the broadcaster, who remains a mystery as far as I know," Katherine said.

"I'll bet it's going to be Peter Dillingham himself," said Georgia. "I just have a feeling."

"Peter would be perfect. He's got a great radio voice, and no one knows more about Old Hawaii than Dillingham," Gordon added.

The Sullivan's and the Grant's ate and tried to laugh their way through the evening, but even the warm breeze could not lift the cloud over Derek's fate from their thoughts and conversation. It cast a discernable pall over the evening.

Jack and Katherine had barely pulled out of the Club's driveway when Katherine asked the question she had been thinking about all evening.

"So, my dear, what is the next step in your investigation?"

"Hollywood."

"Hollywood?"

"Hollywood. I'm going to call my old client Bob Street to see what he knows about Derek Reynolds and, more importantly, what he knows about those who knew Reynolds and didn't like him."

"Who is Bob Street?"

"About ten years ago, I represented a company he used to work for and, over the years, we've stayed in touch. He used to practice law but he's a producer now, with his own company, and doing quite well. He also knows the buzz about everything that's going on in Hollywood."

"What do you think you'll get out of him?"

"I don't know yet, but Bob will know something. And you know what else? I'm going to take Sidney Lane up on her invitation to see the Lanes' Hawaiian gardens tomorrow."

CHAPTER
TWENTY TWO

The next morning, Jack got up earlier than he usually did on Saturday, anxious to call Bob Street, whose day in Los Angeles began two hours earlier than Honolulu's. He left Katherine sleeping, showered and dressed, and made the morning pot of Kona coffee. Hearing the floor creak, Jack looked up from the French Press and saw a half-awake Katherine staring at him.

"Morning, handsome, what are you doing?"

"I want to call Bob before he gets too busy."

"But now I'm awake."

"Why did you wake up?"

"Because you weren't there." She stretched languidly, causing her blonde hair to fall over her eyes.

"Then you should join me as I move one step closer to solving the murder of Derek Reynolds."

"You really think he'll know something useful?" Katherine asked as she leaned against Jack at the kitchen counter.

"I do. Bob's a player on the Hollywood scene. Other producers consult him about movies they're thinking about making. They also call him when they're looking for financial backing."

"Haven't I met him?"

"He rarely travels east. We invited him to our wedding but he couldn't come because his girlfriend was sick and he didn't want to leave her."

"Oh, now I remember him. We had dinner with him once when he came east to visit some relatives?"

"That's right. You did meet him."

"I think I'll take a pass on your telephone call and join you for breakfast later."

Jack gathered his thoughts, finished his cup of coffee, and dialed Bob's number in Santa Monica. It was seven-thirty in Los Angeles and, unless he was out at a film shoot, Bob would still be home.

"Hello," said the familiar voice at the other end of the line.

"Bob, this is Jack Sullivan, how are you?"

"Hey, Jack. I'm fine. How's your Hawaiian adventure going?"

"It's going great. I've got the coffee plantation up and running."

"You know, Jack, I still can't believe you did it. You must be the only guy in the western hemisphere to leave a partnership at a big law firm for the insanity and insecurity of the commodities market."

"It was time for new challenges."

"I know what you mean. Nearly every lawyer I know here in L.A. will tell you after one drink how much he wants to get out of it."

"You hear a lot of that these days, but I can't complain. It was good to me. I probably wouldn't be out here if I hadn't done that first."

"Well, hell, with your talent, you can always go back to it if you want to. So, what can I do for you?"

"Bob, do you know or, I guess I should say, did you know Derek Reynolds?"

"Yes, I knew him quite well. What interests you about Derek? Are you working on a case?"

"Sort of. I'll fill you in later."

"Well, I'll tell you, I was stunned by his death over in your part of the world. In fact, my first thought was that he'd be alive today if he hadn't decided to film part of that movie on Oahu. But then I realized it might not have mattered, because the other movie he was thinking about making was also set in Hawaii."

"How do you know so much about the movies he was making?"

"He asked me to take a look at two screenplays he'd read and liked. Frankly, I think he wanted me to join him as a financial partner as much as to get my thoughts on the screenplays."

"Did you read them?"

"Yeah, I read both of them and I preferred the one he decided not to make. I thought he made a mistake. So did his wife."

"Who's his wife?"

"Loretta Anderson Reynolds."

"Wasn't she an actress a long time ago?"

"Yep, she gave up her career when she married Derek, but she's a very smart lady with an eye for scripts. She reviewed every screenplay Derek got hold of, and he relied on her advice."

"How did it happen that both you and Loretta preferred one screenplay and Derek chose the other one?"

"He ignored our advice. Frankly, I think he chose the screenplay he did, because the main romantic character in it was a better fit for Hypatia Adams. Derek's been fooling around with her for the past year."

"Did Loretta know about that?"

"She did, and she was very unhappy about it, but there wasn't much she could do. It wasn't the first time Derek had been off the reservation, but he was seriously off it with Hypatia. And I think that, in response, Loretta went off the reservation a bit too. Pretty Hollywood-sounding, huh?"

"Why did you like the other screenplay?"

"Jack, it was a classic Alfred Hitchcock-type murder mystery. Too many movies today are either violent or saccharine. Noise has become the primary experience for moviegoers. That and teenage sexual escapades. There's not enough sophistication and elegance anymore. Look at any Hitchcock film and that's what you see — elegant and attractive people in beautiful places engaged in suspense, deception, and skulduggery. The characters are well-dressed, polite and interesting and they're involved in compelling stories. The screenplay Loretta and I liked had all of those elements, but the one Derek chose was just a sappy love story. It'll probably be moderately successful but it won't have any lasting value."

"You mean I'm not likely to see it featured in a film festival in ten years."

"I guarantee you that it will soon be collecting dust in the backs of video stores."

"Did Derek have any enemies in Hollywood? I mean did anyone have an axe to grind with him?"

"Derek was not a warm and cuddly guy. He was a very tough businessman who pissed off a lot of people in this business, both here and in New York. He wasn't loyal to others in the business who had worked very hard for him, and he never lifted a finger to help any of the young people in his production companies. He used people and threw them away. When he made his bundle, he pulled up the drawbridge and let everyone else figure out how to cross the moat on their own."

"Sounds like a great guy. I'm sorry I missed the chance to have him over for dinner."

"If you had invited him for dinner, two things would have occurred. First, you'd have heard all night about how great a producer he is. And second, he would not have reciprocated. It would never have occurred to him that he should invite you to dinner. He was the most self-centered man I ever dealt with in this or any other business."

"Well, that's saying something. Your career has traversed the law, the investment business, and now the movies."

"Don't remind me. It makes me feel old."

"It should make you feel wise."

"That I am, but it has come at a high price, my friend."

"I'm afraid that wisdom is the most expensive commodity on the market, Bob. I think Aeschylus said that it comes only after sustained pain and anxiety."

"Well said, Jack. That's why I always enjoy talking with you. You bring out my classical side. But to get back to your question, plenty of people had axes to grind with Derek Reynolds. And I'll guarantee you that very few tears were shed when the news of his demise reached Hollywood. Having said that, I don't know anybody who was so pissed off at Derek that he would have done him in."

"That's helpful, Bob. Thanks. So, are you coming out here anytime soon?"

"I don't have any plans in the immediate future. You should come to L.A. I've done some work on my house, and I now have a spectacular view of Santa Monica beach from my deck. Bring your lovely wife and stay for the weekend."

"I will. By the way, is anybody planning to make a movie out of that other murder mystery you mentioned?"

"Not that I'm aware of, but I've been thinking about calling Loretta after the dust settles to see what ownership Derek may have had in it. You don't see classic 'murder by poison in beautiful settings' anymore."

"Murder by poison?"

"Yes, the screenplay was fascinating. The victim was killed when his drink was poisoned by a completely unknown, very exotic poison."

"What was the name of the poison?"

"I don't remember. It's nothing I'd ever heard of before.

I do remember it sounded like the name of a car."

"A car?"

"Yeah, a foreign car if my memory serves me correctly. If I get hold of the screenplay, I'll check it out and call you."

"Thanks, Bob. It was great talking to you, and we'll try to get over to see you soon."

"I'm counting on it. See you soon, Jack."

The look on Jack's face when he hung up the phone told Katherine that Bob had supplied him with very significant information.

"Katherine, wait till you hear this."

Over breakfast on their lanai, Jack told her about the two screenplays set in Hawaii and the plot of the murder mystery.

"Where do you go from here, Jack?"

"I'm going to the Windward Shore to visit the florist who supplies Jennifer with tropical flowers and plants, and then I'm going to visit the Lane's to see their extensive tropical gardens."

CHAPTER
TWENTY THREE

In light of Gordon Grant's admonition at dinner the previous evening, Jack decided to do some paddling before he tackled the Kailua florist and the Lanes' gardens. On his way to the Diamond Head Canoe Club, he called the Lane's and Sidney answered the phone.

"Sidney, I'm on my way to Kailua to run some errands and I thought I'd call and see if it would be convenient to drop by and see your gardens."

"That would be wonderful, Jack. George has gone to the nursery to select some new plants, but I'm sure he'd love to see you. Why don't you join us for lunch on our lanai and then we'll give you a tour."

"I'd love to. What time would you like me to be there?"

"Why don't you drop by at one o'clock. George should be back by then."

"That's fine, Sidney. I'll see you at one."

Jack turned into the Club's driveway and parked his Jeep in the garage, where the Club's senior bartender was also just arriving.

"Good morning, Kulani. Have they found that jerk who ran you off the road near Kailua yet?"

"No, but they found the car."

"Really. Who owns it?"

"Like I thought, it was a rental car."

"Well, I'm sure the police can find out who was renting it the night it hit your car."

"I don't know. The car that hit me was stolen."

"Was it stolen from someone who had rented it or from the rental agency?"

"It was stolen from the company that rented it. That's the amazing thing. It was Derek Reynolds' production company that rented it."

"No kidding. When did they report it stolen?"

"According to the police, they rented about ten cars for the cast and crew and didn't keep track of them. They didn't even know it was stolen until the police told them."

"So the police found it abandoned somewhere, ran the plates, and discovered that it had been rented by Reynolds' company?"

"Yeah."

"Well, at least you know who to call to get reimbursed for the damage to your car."

"Yeah, they got plenty of insurance, but I want to know who whacked me for no reason."

"I can well understand that. Who did they rent it from?"

"Aloha Transportation out at the airport."

"Was it a Ford Taurus like you thought?"

"Yeah, I guess my eyes are still pretty good."

"I'm sure they are, Kulani. The way you mix drinks in perfect proportion, they'd have to be."

"Thank you, Mr. Sullivan."

Jack entered the locker room, made a beeline for the phone on the trainer's desk, and dialed Dave McNeil's number at Police Headquarters.

"McNeil," Dave's easily recognizable voice announced after the first ring.

"Dave, Jack."

"I'm sorry, old buddy, but I don't have the lab results yet. I'll call you as soon as I hear from Dr. Wong."

"That's not what I'm calling about."

"Have you been doing some more sleuthing?"

"Sort of. Dave, I have a hunch, and my instincts have always been pretty good."

"No doubt about that, Jack. You expose yourself to abuse from the golf god a lot less than I do."

"I've been giving this case a lot of thought, Dave, and I'd appreciate it if you'd check something out for me."

"What is it?"

"The bartender at the Club on Monday night was Kulani."

"I know Kulani well. He's usually in the position of consoling me after Grant kicks my ass on the links."

"Well, on Tuesday night, after Kulani closed the bar and cleaned up at the Club, he was driving home to Kailua, when somebody ran him off the road on to the beach near Lanikai. He thought someone was trying to kill him."

"Not just another wild kid heading home after a night on the town?"

"No. Kulani got a look at the driver, and he doesn't think it was a local."

"Did he report it to the police?"

"Yes, and your crack department found the car. It had been stolen and then abandoned. They traced it to the Aloha Transportation Company out at the airport."

"Who rented it from Aloha?"

"It was one of several cars that Derek Reynolds' production company had rented for the duration of the film shoot."

"And let me guess. They didn't even know it was stolen until our guys told them, right?"

"You got it."

"That must be what the guys from auto theft want to talk to me about. They called me a few hours ago and wanted to set up a meeting. But I've been so damn busy dealing with these interviews of everybody who was at the Club on Monday night that I haven't had time to get back to them. So, Jack, what can I do for you?"

"I want you to compare the tire treads on the car that hit Kulani with the tread marks I photographed in that field near Kailua, where the 'Akia was growing."

"Don't you think that's a long shot?"

"It probably is, but there are just too many strange coincidences occurring around Kailua. And they all have one common element."

"What's that?"

"They all involve people who, one way or another, were around Derek Reynolds when he was here. I'll lay it all out for you as soon as I get a few more facts."

"Well, I'll go you one better, Jack. I was so impressed with your photographs that I sent one of our crime scene search teams out to the field where you found that 'Akia and told them to sweep it and take plaster casts of those tire tracks."

"I thought my evidence had made an impression on you. Pun intended. Dave, I really think I'm on to something. I'll call you later today to get the lab results."

"Thanks. Just don't get yourself crosswise with the wrong person. That's what we're here for. And Jack, just between you and me and without getting into any of the details, my guys have learned a lot about the Lane's in the last few days. And they're looking into some relationships that Derek had with other people who were at the party. You know what I mean?"

"I hear you. I'll be careful. And one more thing, Dave. When your forensic guys examine the tire treads on that rental car, will you ask them to sweep the car for prints and any other evidence?"

"I'll make sure they do."

Jack hung up the phone, more convinced than ever that the dots he was connecting would lead to the murderer. He undressed, put his paddling gear on, and went outside to his canoe, which hung in the rack farthest from the beach, the result of seniority rules at the Club. He decided to do a power workout and paddled straight out for two miles at a high rate of strokes per minute and then repeated the run back to the beach at the same speed. His heart was pounding, and stinging salty sweat poured into his eyes, but the prospect of solving the case infused him with energy as he surfed onto the beach at the Club. Jack looked at his watch and knew that he had just enough time to visit the florist in Kailua before he was due at the Lanes.

CHAPTER
TWENTY FOUR

Jack decided to take the Pali Highway across the southeastern part of Oahu, through the Koolau Mountains, to the Windward Shore town of Kailua. The Koolaus dominate the eastern side of Oahu, and their verdant peaks were shrouded in mist as Jack emerged from the tunnel cut through the mountains and headed for the Windward Shore a short distance away.

Fifteen minutes later, he was in the town of Kailua, looking for a parking spot on Kailua Road near the florist's shop. Tropical Flora looked small from the outside but, as Jack entered, he saw that it stretched far back into the property and featured a backyard filled with plants of all sizes, colors and shapes.

"Good morning, sir, can I help you?" an elderly Hawaiian man asked.

"Yes. I'm interested in tropical plants that are native to the islands."

"Anything in particular?"

"I'd like to take a look at some of your ornamental shrubs."

"Come with me. They're out back."

Jack followed the old man through a colorful jungle. Flowers in every shade of red, pink, coral and yellow were arranged on wooden shelves nearly seven feet high along one side of the narrow store. The shelves on the opposite side held only white flowers – white Anthuriums and Bougainvillea, Gardenias, Ginger, Hibiscus and Orchids — that looked like a wave breaking toward the red Anthuriums and Bougainvillea, Ginger, Hibiscus, Royal Poinciana, Heliconias and Begonias.

"I've never seen so many flowers in one place," Jack said as he reached the open yard at the back of the store.

"Yes, we supply flowers to people all over the world. Hawaii's flowers are in great demand."

"Actually, the reason I came here was because a friend of my wife sent her some flowers and plants from your shop and I was very impressed."

"Who would that be?"

"Jennifer Adams."

"Oh, Jennifer. She's one of my best customers. Thanks to her, Los Angeles is my biggest market. Jennifer has introduced my flowers and plants to all her Hollywood friends."

"Does she buy a lot of plants from you?"

"Yes, they're mainly used on TV and movie sets. She tells me that my plants are in many movies."

"Well, Jennifer certainly made my wife's dress shop look brighter with your plants."

"I'm not surprised. She's learned quite a lot about Hawaiian plants and flowers and always knows just the right one to put in just the right place."

"How does she know so much about tropical plants?"

"Oh, Jennifer has been studying Hawaiian plants and flowers for several years, and she comes out here once a month to make her selections from my shop. Sometimes I think she knows more about our plants and flowers than I do."

"Do you supply her from here with everything she needs?"

"Pretty much, but Jennifer is very resourceful. She drives around the island looking for new plants and flowers that I don't have and asks me to get them for her."

"Well, there certainly are a lot of plants and flowers on these islands. You could spend a lifetime here and not see them all."

"You're quite right about that, sir. I see new ones all the time that I never noticed before, and I've lived here all my life. Now, what would you like to see that I either have here or can get for you?"

"As I said, I'm interested in ornamental shrubs, and one that has been recommended to me is 'Akia."

"I'm surprised to hear you say that. 'Akia is not one of Hawaii's more beautiful ornamental shrubs, but I am familiar with it. May I recommend something a little more colorful and taller?"

"Do you have any 'Akia that I could take a look at?"

"No, I've got lots of other ornamentals, but no 'Akia."

"Not much demand for it, huh?"

"I can't recall anyone asking me for it."

"Does it grow anywhere around here, so I could take a look at it?"

"I've seen it in fields between the town and the beach. Do you know what it looks like?"

"Do you have a picture of it?"

"Let me get my guide to tropical plants and flowers and see if I can find it for you."

"Oh, that's all right, maybe I should consider something else."

"No, here it is; there's a photograph in my book."

Jack looked at the color photograph of an 'Akia bush and silently agreed with the florist that it would not be his first choice for an ornamental shrub.

"Well, thanks very much for your time. I think I'll drive out toward the beach and see if I can find an 'Akia bush and figure out whether I really want to use it as an ornamental."

"As you drive toward the beach, look for any open field and you'll probably find one. Let me know if I can help you in any other way."

"I will. Oh, I should ask you something before I go looking for 'Akia. Is there anything I should know about it? Is it dangerous like the Angel's Trumpet flowers?"

"I wouldn't eat it. There's an old Hawaiian legend that says it's poisonous, but I've never run into anyone who's had a problem with it."

"Thanks. I'm sure I'll be back."

"Goodbye sir and good luck."

Well, Jack thought, Jennifer is very knowledgeable about Hawaiian plants. And her wholesaler knows about 'Akia. He wondered what his visit to the Lane's would bring and decided to take the beach road and check out the fields along the way. The Lane's lived in Lanikai, an upscale area on the coast just south of Kailua. As he drove along Lanikai Beach Road toward their house, Jack realized that he was again close to the place where Kulani had been run off the road and not far from the field where he had found the poisonous 'Akia.

The Lane's lived in a large white house with a portico and pillars that gave it an air of royalty. It reminded Jack of Washington Place, the official residence of Hawaii's governors in downtown Honolulu. He imagined that, with its broad porch and overhanging roof, the Lanes' house might have been like those that Hawaiian royalty had built at Waikiki in the late nineteenth century. As Jack approached the house, Sidney came down from the porch to meet him.

"Good afternoon, Jack."

"Hello, Sidney. What a house! I thought Princess Kaiulani might come out to greet me."

"You are so kind. George and I tried to make it as beautiful and comfortable as we could in an Old Hawaii sort of way."

"Well, I've only seen the porch but I'd say you've succeeded."

"Let me show you inside. We'll be having lunch on the lanai out back as soon as George arrives."

The walls of the living room and dining room were covered in panels made of Hawaii's most valuable koa wood, a clear sign of the house's age and quality. This much koa had not been available at reasonable prices since the early part of the twentieth century. The moldings around the door frames and the mantel that framed the fireplace reminded Jack of old beach cottages on the east coast that had also been built in the 1920's.

"Jack, you must see our library."

"I'd love to," Jack said as he walked through the living room to an adjoining room that was also richly appointed and elegant.

"You've got a huge library here," Jack exclaimed as he surveyed floor to ceiling mahogany shelves that were packed with row after row of books.

"George and I have a fondness for the nineteenth century, when books were the major form of entertainment. That may surprise you, since we were both in the movie business for so long."

"It does surprise me!"

"I thought it would. I'll tell you why over lunch."

"May I look at some of your books?"

"Certainly. In fact, since you're developing an interest in tropical plants and flowers, let me show you our collection of botanical references."

Sidney took Jack to one corner of the library by a window that looked out on the Lanes' expansive gardens and waved her hand across row after row of books about plants and flowers found in the islands.

"I feel like I'm in the Bishop Museum," Jack said turning to Sidney.

"You might as well be. I don't mean to boast, but our collection is nearly as extensive as theirs."

"Do you also have books about Hawaiian culture and tradition, like the Museum does?"

"Of course, they're right over here," she said, pointing to a group of shelves adjacent to those that held the botanical treatises.

"For ease of reference, I assume," said Jack.

"Yes, one subject does lead naturally to the other. When you study Hawaiian customs, you must also learn about their plants and flowers."

"You've really gotten into this, haven't you Sidney?"

"Yes, we have. It's been sort of an escape for George and me from an unhappy period in our lives."

Just then, the front door opened and Jack heard George Lane's voice.

"Sidney, I'm home."

Sidney led Jack out of the library and back into the living room where she waved to George, who was colorfully attired in a green linen sport coat, yellow pants, and a pink shirt punctuated with a paisley ascot.

"Sorry I'm late, Sidney. I stopped by the marina to talk to the mechanic about the boat. Damn engine's been giving me problems. Good Afternoon, Jack. I see Sidney's giving you the cook's tour of our archives."

"Yes, and I must say that I've enjoyed it. Your house is beautiful, George, and your library is fascinating."

"I'm glad you like it. Sidney tells me you're developing an interest in all things Hawaiian."

"I am. Katherine and I want to make these islands home, so we're trying to learn everything we can about them."

"That's just the way we felt when we started out here."

"Lunch is served on the lanai," Sidney announced from the kitchen.

George led Jack out to an elegant patio a few steps down from the back door of the house. Sidney had set a table for three with a linen tablecloth and her finest china and silver.

"Sidney, this looks beautiful. Than you for having me to such an elegant lunch."

"It's our pleasure, Jack. George and I liked you and Katherine the first time we met you at the Grant's, and we're just thrilled that you enjoy the islands as much as we do."

"We really do love it here," Jack said as he sat down. "We feel completely at home, even though we're thousands of miles away from where we grew up."

"The islands have that effect on some people," George said as he sat down. "It's hard to tell who will be comfortable here, but I can see that you are."

"I am. Katherine and I really love it here."

"I told Jack about our interest in botany, dear, and about our collection of books."

"Jack", George said, "the older I get, the fonder I become of the past. We came here to get away from our life in Hollywood. It was a terrible place for us, full of lies, backstabbing, and double-dealing. We reached the point where we hated getting up in the morning and going to work in the movie business. It was one duplicitous person after another, and the worst part was that, because of their positions, these people were able to control us in all kinds of ways, not the least of which was our livelihood. So one day, after we experienced the proverbial straw that broke the camel's back, we decided we'd had enough and left."

"And we've been ecstatically happy here ever since," Sidney said.

"Yes, with only one exception", George added.

"What was that?" Jack asked.

"When we saw Derek Reynolds at the Club on Monday night. It brought back all the bad memories."

"Had you worked with him?"

"Yes, Sidney did, and he told her he would make her a star, but he always found another actress who was more useful to him for other reasons. He let us down time after time."

"Enough of that, dear, you shouldn't speak ill of the dead," Sidney said.

"Good riddance as far as I'm concerned."

"Oh stop, George. God will send a bolt of lightning if you don't."

"I doubt it. I'm sure He shares my view, especially since He knows a lot more about Derek than I do, and I'm sure none of it is good."

During their luncheon conversation, Jack noticed that the index and middle fingers on George's right hand bore the unmistakable yellow stains of tobacco. And his right thumb tended toward a shade of brown that was not the result of exposure to the Central Pacific sun.

"Jack", Sidney said, "let's go out to the garden. I want you to see it before that bolt of lightning strikes!"

Sidney and George took Jack on an hour-long tour of their garden. There were formal areas near the house and wild ones near the edge of the property. Sidney and George knew the identity of every flower and plant and the role of each in Hawaiian culture and traditions. In one corner at the far edge of their property, Jack spotted a familiar looking bush next to an empty patch of soil that looked freshly tilled.

"Is that an 'Akia?" Jack inquired.

George turned quickly, looking directly at Jack.

"You've been studying, haven't you?" he asked.

"Yes, I have. I'm trying to get a handle on as many native plants as possible." Jack tried his best to appear nonchalant.

"How do you know about 'Akia?" George asked with a furrowed brow.

"Oh, I read about it in one of the botanical treatises and I've seen it around the island."

"It's not one of the more desirable ornamentals but it is native to Oahu, so we thought we ought to have it in our garden." George spoke in a sharp tone that conveyed a distinct desire to change the subject.

"Yes, there are a lot more that are better looking," Jack said.

"But it was present in traditional Hawaiian gardens," George added.

"Really?" Jack exclaimed.

"Yes, 'Akia was a popular shrub and it's still seen all over the island."

"Well, maybe I'll look into getting some for our place on the Big Island. It's not dangerous is it, George?"

"I've never heard of anyone getting sick from touching it."

"How about eating it? Are there any dangerous parts that you shouldn't eat?"

"I don't know. As I said, I've never known anyone to get sick from contact with 'Akia."

"I'll give it some thought, but you're right, there are lots of better looking ornamentals."

"Many more, Jack," Sidney said. "Come with me and I'll show you some of them, as well as our flowers."

She showed him a raucous array of Bougainvillea, Royal Poinciana, Hibiscus, Anthuriums, Plumeria, and Oleander.

"You have to be careful with Oleander, Jack. It can make you sick," Sidney said.

"Yes, I've learned about a few of the dangerous plants in my reading. In fact, I'm happy to see you don't have any Angel's Trumpets."

"No, they are very dangerous. And we don't have any Be-Still trees either. I don't want our cat and dog chewing them, and I don't want any children tasting them either."

"That about does it, Jack," George announced as they reached the point where they had begun their tour. "I hope you'll bring Katherine over some time."

"I will, and thank you both for a lovely afternoon. Maybe you could visit us on the Big Island some time and tell us what you think we should plant around our house over there. I could also show you around the Plantation."

"We'd love to. George and I try to get over to The Poinciana one weekend a month, but we don't get over nearly often enough."

"Not nearly enough," George added gratuitously.

"Well, please be sure to call and let me know the next time you're going over."

"I shall. Goodbye, Jack," said Sidney.

Jack decided to take the long way back to the Royal Hawaiian and drove from the Lanes' house on Lanikai Beach Road to Kalanianaole Highway. Before long, however, the traffic slowed to a crawl because of road repairs ahead, and the delay gave Jack time to think about the day's events. He was careful not to make linkages where there was insufficient evidence and resisted drawing conclusions before all the facts were in, but he could not discount the fact that there were three people at the party — Jennifer Adams and George and Sidney Lane — who had good reason to wish Derek Reynolds ill. And each of them probably knew about the toxic properties of 'Akia.

Jennifer probably knew where to find the toxic strain of 'Akia from her explorations around the island of Oahu, searching for plants for her Hollywood clients. And Jack could not get the sight of that empty patch of freshly-tilled soil next to the 'Akia shrubs at the back of the Lanes' garden out of his mind. He also thought it unlikely that George Lane, with the most complete collection of books about Hawaiian plants, customs and rituals outside the walls of the Bishop Museum, had not researched every plant before placing it in his garden and did not know about the legendary Hawaiian ceremony in which 'Akia shrubs were used as a source of poison for the execution of criminals. And George, with his tobacco-stained fingers, had seemed damned uncomfortable during the garden tour when the talk turned to 'Akia.

Traffic moved at a snail's pace for ten minutes, causing Jack to turn his attention to the scenery. As his gaze shifted from the houses along the highway to the long line of vehicles in front of him, his eyes stopped at the chrome letters inside the oval on the trunk of the car in front of him, identifying its Korean manufacturer.

The car was a Kia.

CHAPTER TWENTY FIVE

Jack reached for his cell phone on the passenger seat of the Jeep and realized that he had turned it off when he arrived at the Lane's. As soon as he turned it back on, the phone buzzed and the carrier's monotone voice informed him that he had received one message. That voice was immediately followed by Dave McNeil's one-word message:

"Bingo!"

Jack was elated. Dave's communiqué, delivered in a secure code over cell phone air waves, told Jack all he needed to know until he could get to a land line and talk to Dave privately. The lab analyses had concluded that the toxic fluid found in Derek Reynolds' stomach had come from the 'Akia plant. Jack immediately called Katherine at her dress shop.

"Hellooo," he crowed into the phone as soon as he heard Katherine pick it up.

"Hi, hubby. What's new?"

"Well, I've just had a very interesting and productive day, and I want to tell you all about it. In fact, I'm hoping I can persuade you to close up early and meet me at home."

"I think that can be arranged. How far are you from home now?"

"I'm about twenty minutes away if this traffic doesn't jam up again."

"I'll be there, Jack."

Jack's estimate was right on the mark. Twenty minutes later, at 3:30, he pulled into the driveway of the Royal Hawaiian. He covered the thirty feet between the lobby's entrance and the elevators in a few seconds, jumped into a closing elevator, and ran up the half flight of stairs to their tower suite. Katherine had not yet arrived, so Jack decided to call Dave and get the details about the lab tests.

"McNeil."

"Dave, Jack. I got your message on my cell phone."

"You were right, old boy. Dr. Wong called me early this afternoon with the results of the lab tests comparing the contents of Reynolds' stomach with fluid from that bush you brought us. They match."

"I felt it in my bones, Dave. I just knew it."

"Well, I've always said you've got great instincts."

"Damn!"

"There's more, Jack."

"What else did you find?"

"The lab took a closer look at the stomach fluids and found some particles in the contents of Reynolds' stomach that could also be traced to 'Akia. They're pieces of bark and leaves that were probably ground in during the process of extracting fluid from the plant."

"So, you've got a positive identification of the poison."

"Yes, we do. The toxicologists are very excited. They've never seen this one before."

"Well, it's just like Papa David told me. You might only see it once in a lifetime."

"He's a wise man. I should put him on the payroll."

"You should at least consult him, Dave. Who knows what other crimes he could help you solve or even prevent."

"You're right. But, at the moment, it looks like you're the one who's helping me solve crimes."

"I'm just an amateur."

"I disagree, Jack. I haven't told you what else we've found."

"There's more?"

"I had my boys impound the Ford Taurus that was stolen from Reynolds' production company, and the forensic team had a double-header."

"What did they find?"

"When they compared the treads on the Taurus's tires with the plaster casts of the tread marks from the mud out in Kailua where you found that 'Akia, they got two hits. They got a match for that class of tire — you know, the same tread design, size and manufacturer. And they got an individual match for each tire tread. The knicks and cuts in each of the Taurus's tires showed up in the plaster casts of the tread marks from the field."

"No kidding."

"Nope."

"Why do I have the feeling that you have more?"

"Because I do. My boys also searched the Taurus thoroughly. They gave it the full crime scene treatment and found some very interesting things."

"Like what?"

"Remnants of leaves and twigs in the trunk that sure look like that 'Akia bush you brought in here."

"Holy shit!"

"There's more. Among the various cigarette butts in the car's ashtray was a Camel, just like the one you found under the 'Akia shrub. Sort of like another present under the Christmas tree, if you catch my drift."

"Can you do a DNA analysis on it?"

"We're examining both Camels to see whether we've got sufficient DNA material to perform an analysis."

"That's great, Dave."

"Maybe, maybe not. There might still be a problem, even if we have enough DNA to identify its characteristics."

"Why?"

"Because the national data bank of DNA characteristics is small compared with the national data bank of fingerprints. Congress passed a law in 2006 that lets the feds collect DNA samples from anyone they've arrested, just like they do with fingerprints, but they've got a long way to go to catch up with the fingerprint data."

"I see. You may be able to identify a set of DNA characteristics but not be able to match them with anyone, because that person's DNA characteristics are not contained in the national data bank."

"Right. And if you don't have anything to match that evidence with, you don't have any useful evidence."

"So you need to find the person whose DNA matches the characteristics you get from the cigarette butts."

"Correctamundo."

"How about fingerprints?"

"I thought you'd never ask. The car was loaded with fingerprints, which is no surprise because so many people have used it and touched it. But our crime scene search team is, at this very minute, trying to determine how many discrete sets of prints they can lift from the car."

"Well, I'm still working on some other leads. And I may have something more for you tomorrow."

"Keep at it, Jack, and you'll have my job before you know it. In fact, we could switch jobs. I'd love to run that coffee plantation of yours."

"I'm afraid you'd be a lot better at the coffee business than I'd be at the police business, at least from the City of Honolulu's perspective."

"I'm willing to give it a try, Jack. By the way, we informed Mrs. Reynolds that we can now release the deceased's body to her. She's flying in from Los Angeles tomorrow to escort the body back to California for burial."

"Really? Are you going to meet with her?"

"Right again, Jack. Call me when you have something."

"I will."

Katherine walked into the kitchen as Jack hung up the phone.

"That is a Cheshire cat grin if I have ever seen one, my dear."

"I prefer to call it a Maine Coon grin," Jack said.

"Tell me about your day," Katherine said as she flopped down on the sofa next to Jack.

Jack proceeded to recount the entire day, starting with his encounter with Kulani at the Club when he learned about the Ford Taurus, running through his discussion with the Kailua florist about Jennifer, to his lunch at the Lane's and the tour of their gardens with the empty patch of freshly turned soil next to the 'Akia shrubs, to the Kia car in front of him on Kalanianaole Highway, and ending with his conversation with Dave McNeil about the results of the toxicology analysis and the evidence found in the Ford Taurus.

"Jack, I knew you were on to something but now I know you're really going to solve this crime!"

"I am. But I still need more information and I know just where I'm going to get it."

"Where?"

"Bob Street."

"You didn't get it all out of him this morning?"

"I didn't know everything this morning that I know now. So I've got some more questions for him."

"When are you going to call him?"

"Right now, I've got to strike while the iron's hot."

"What do you think about pizza for dinner?"

"Perfect! I think it's going to be that kind of an evening."

"I'll call and tell them to deliver it around 8 o'clock."

"Great! Maybe we can even get a swim in first."

"I'll order the usual – onions, olives and tomato slices."

"I can taste it now."

While Katherine called the local pizzeria, Jack gathered his thoughts. If the poison used in the screenplay that Derek rejected was 'Akia, and if that screenplay was all over Hollywood, then the list of possible suspects could be extensive. If its circulation was limited, the list of suspects would be smaller. Maybe very small.

"I'm off the phone, Jack, and dinner is all set. You can call Bob now."

Jack dialed Bob Street's number in Santa Monica and got lucky again.

"Bob, this is Jack."

"Are you still on that case?"

"I am and I've got some more questions for you. Listen, do you remember telling me that the poison used in the Alfred Hitchcock-type screenplay sounded like the name of a foreign car?"

"Yep."

"Was that car a Kia?"

"You know, I think it was. That's a Korean car, isn't it?"

"Yes. I saw one today and made the connection with a plant out here that's poisonous."

"I'll be damned. I should probably check the screenplay but, now that I think about it, I'm sure the poison was 'Akia."

"Have you by any chance spoken with Loretta about the legal status of that screenplay?"

"I called her on Tuesday to convey my condolences but I didn't have the heart to bring up business."

"I can certainly understand that. Did that screenplay get wide circulation in L.A.?"

"I don't think so. I haven't heard anybody talk about it. The only people I know who read it were Derek, Loretta and me. By the way, Jack, Loretta's flying out to Honolulu tomorrow to pick up Derek's remains. She called and invited me to the funeral."

"Was she upset?"

"I only spoke with her for a few minutes but, yes, I would say she sounded upset."

"This must have set off a lot of emotions, what with Derek being out here with Hypatia when he died."

"No doubt about that. I'm sure she was angry and jealous and I'm sure her anger was directed as much at Hypatia as at Derek."

"Well, it couldn't have been all that bad, Bob. You said Loretta has been off the reservation herself a few times."

"The difference is that her dalliances were only in response to Derek's, and they were never really serious. She'd latch on to some young actor, sort of the way a woman vacationing at a spa might find a pool boy for a little entertainment."

"Who's her current latchee?"

"I don't know. I'm not even sure she has one at the moment. But if she does, she'll keep him in the background. Loretta is very discreet."

"If she had one, would she bring him to Honolulu to claim Derek's remains?"

"I doubt it. Loretta wouldn't want to risk the kind of impression that would make. She's rather proper."

"Well, if you get a look at that screenplay again, double check the name of the poison and give me a call."

"I will, Jack, but the more I think about it, the more certain I am that it was 'Akia. I remember associating the poison with the car when I read it. I'll call you if I get hold of it."

"Thanks, Bob," Jack said as he hung up and began to sketch out notes of everything he had learned to date.

Two hours later, after a quick dip in the Pacific, the doorbell rang and the smell of pizza filled the living room. Jack made a beeline to the refrigerator for a Miller Lite — in his view the perfect partner for this entrée — and joined Katherine on their lanai.

"What did you learn from Bob this time?"

"In the screenplay that Derek Reynolds was reviewing, 'Akia was the poison."

"Really? And who else read that screenplay?"

"The only other person Bob knows who read it, besides himself and Derek, was Loretta."

"So, since Loretta wasn't at the cast party on Monday night, you need to find out whether Bob is correct that no one else read it."

"Exactly."

"How are you going to do that?"

"I've been pondering that very question since I hung up the phone. And I think I have the answer, or at least the starting point."

"And that is?"

"Breakfast with Arthur Fairbanks tomorrow morning."

CHAPTER
TWENTY SIX

There is no more enjoyable restaurant for breakfast than the Surf Room at the Royal Hawaiian Hotel. Situated on the edge of Waikiki Beach, it offers a panoramic view of the world's most famous beach. Jack arrived there at eight-thirty and, while waiting for Arthur Fairbanks, picked up a fax copy of the Sunday *New York Times* from a table at the entrance to the restaurant and scanned the front page.

"Good morning, my good man," Arthur intoned with a slight nod of the head. "Very sorry I'm late. The lifts were a bit slow this morning."

"That's all right, Arthur. I just got here myself. How have you been?"

"I've been tip top. Dillingham has been pestering me about his bloody radio show but, other than that, I have no complaints."

"Yes, he's very excited about it, and Katherine and I are looking forward to it."

"I must admit that I am as well."

Just then, Lily, the hostess, dressed in a long pink dress imprinted with white flowers, approached them.

"Good Morning, Mr. Sullivan, Mr. Fairbanks. Would you like a table by the beach?"

Jack nodded, and they followed her through the interior of the Surf Room, beneath the pink and white awning that covers its porch, to a table next to the low pink wall that separates the porch from sand that stretches in a crescent from Waikiki to Diamond Head.

"Lily, have you added bangers and mash to the breakfast menu yet?"

"No, Mr. Fairbanks. I talked with the chef about your request, but he's sticking with American and Japanese breakfast entrees for now."

"A continuing tragedy, Lily, and one that leaves me no alternative but to resort to my usual poached eggs on toast, with some Earl Grey tea, please."

"I'll have guava juice, mango with slices of lime, whole wheat toast and coffee, Lily," said Jack. "Arthur, I've been thinking about this Derek Reynolds thing and trying to figure it out."

"What are you bolluxed about? I realize that the police are buggering everyone who was at the party, but do you have reason to believe it was anything other than a heart attack — the byproduct of his lifestyle over the past thirty years."

"Do you know Derek's wife Loretta, Arthur?"

"Yes, I've known her for quite a long time, since she burst on to the Hollywood scene as what they used to call an ingénue."

"What's she like?"

"She was a very talented young actress. A very attractive blonde, which I'm sure won't surprise you."

"How old is she?"

"Loretta is probably in her mid-to late-forties now. They've been married about twenty years."

"That's strange. I've never seen any of her movies. Was she mostly a stage actress?"

"No, she was a screen actress, but she didn't make many movies."

"Why not, if she was so talented?"

"Because Derek didn't want her to work. He wanted a full-time wife, or so he told her at the time."

"What do you mean by that?"

"He gave her the old American line that he wanted her to be the mother of his children and didn't want her running off from one movie set to another, which she could have done quite easily given her talent and her beauty."

"What did he really want?"

"It's what he didn't want, Jack. He didn't want any competition."

"He feared competition from Loretta?"

"Competition may not be the right word. He wanted a beautiful and talented wife but not one who, because of her own accomplishments, might attract attention and draw it away from him. So Derek made a deal with Loretta. In return for giving up her career, he would give her a very comfortable life with a big house and lots of money."

"And she cut that deal?"

"Yes, she did. Loretta grew up on the wrong side of the castle, or as you Yanks say, the tracks. She was poor and had a very difficult childhood. Her parents' home was in disarray all the time, and it's remarkable that she emerged from it at all."

"Wouldn't that make her even more reluctant to give up her career?"

"Not really. Think about it, Jack. Actors and actresses lead very insecure lives. They don't know when the next call is coming from a producer or director or if any call will ever come."

"But you said she was good."

"She was smashing, but she knew how harsh the world could be, and she didn't want to risk returning to a life of poverty under any circumstances. And besides, Jack, you know it doesn't necessarily matter whether you're good or not. The law business is not that different from the acting business. A lot depends on who you know. It's the very essence of the personal services industry."

"Did Derek live up to his side of the bargain?"

"He did and he didn't. As Mrs. Derek Reynolds, she had plenty of money but she didn't have security, which was always of more concern to Loretta."

"What do you mean?"

"Well, once she gave up her career, Derek knew he had her in a bind. She couldn't go back to it, because her best years were gone. And the longer she stayed out of it, the less interest Hollywood producers and directors had in her."

"So he felt as if he could get away with murder? Sorry for the use of that metaphor, Arthur."

"Actually, my good man, you're quite correct. He continued to provide her with the trappings of wealth but he also kept up his philandering. She was convinced that he would leave her someday."

"It sounds like she'd have been better off if he had.

They'd have gotten divorced and she'd have taken a chunk of his wealth to ease the pain."

"That's probably true, but she always held out hope that he'd change and return only to her. At least until Hypatia arrived on the scene. Derek was insane about Hypatia. She made him crazy. He couldn't think about any other woman after he met her."

"I imagine Loretta didn't react too well to that."

"No, that really pushed her over the edge. For the first time, I began to see her slipping about in public with other men."

"Anybody famous?"

"No, none of the well-known actors would risk incurring the wrath of Derek Reynolds. She was drawn to the up and coming younger set."

"Did you see her out with many of these guys?"

"I wouldn't say many, but there were certainly a few. No one held it against her or even thought less of her, because Derek was rather notorious. He was completely over the top with Hypatia, at least in his pursuit of her."

"What do you mean by that?"

"As I said, Hypatia made Derek completely crazy, but I don't think Derek had the same effect on her. It seemed to me that she tolerated him because, as a professional matter, she had to. I always doubted that anything was really going on between the two of them."

"So what was Loretta worried about?"

"Derek conveyed the impression to everyone in Hollywood that there was quite a lot going on between him and Hypatia. The coup de grace was Derek's selection of the screenplay they're filming here on Oahu and giving Hypatia the lead role. I think he believed this would really get Hypatia's attention. And so did Loretta."

"Did Loretta weigh in on this screenplay?"

"I'm sure she did. She reviewed all of them for him and she was a bloody good critic. She visited her acumen on me a few times, and I was convinced that she should have become a movie producer herself after she left the silver screen."

"Did anyone else review screenplays for Derek?"

"Not that I know of."

"I hear Loretta's coming out to Honolulu today to pick up Derek's body and take him back to Los Angeles for burial. The autopsy has been completed."

"I'd love to see her. I have great respect for her."

"If there's a memorial service here, maybe you can attend."

"I hope so, Jack. It would be a proper gesture from the cast and crew. I think I'll inquire, now that I know Loretta is coming."

"Would you let me know also, Arthur?"

"Of course, and, by the way, have you been out to see the Lanes' gardens?"

"I was out there yesterday afternoon for lunch. You were right on target. They are spectacular."

"Smashing! I'm glad you went. I don't know anyone who has learned more about Hawaiian culture and recreated the atmosphere of Old Hawaii than Sidney and George Lane."

"Yes, I know what you mean. I had a very nice lunch and tour. They seem to have adjusted well to life in the islands."

"Oh, don't be fooled, Jack. They miss the buzz. Sidney follows the movie set like a hawk. She reads every tabloid and movie magazine and subscribes to *Variety*. And she stays in touch with her Hollywood friends by phone. Plus, George is still dabbling in the business."

"I thought he was a banker."

"He's an investment banker who makes a lot of money. And he invests some of it in the movie business."

"Is he very active in it?"

"He still reviews screenplays and gets calls from producers who are looking for financial backing. I dare say he keeps a hand in the business."

"Fascinating."

"That's what I like about you, Jack. You find everything interesting. In a way, you're an explorer, just like Captain Cook."

"That's what my wife says. Well, Arthur, I just looked at my watch and realized that I'm probably cutting into your Sunday schedule."

"Don't worry a bit, Jack. I never fret about losing an hour in the morning because I know I can make it up in the evening. I'm more productive then anyway."

"I feel the same way. I sit down in the evening with Katherine and I come up with ideas much more readily than I do in the morning. Why do you think that is?"

"I'm not sure. If you were coming up with more creative thoughts after one of your famous Wiki Wiki's, I could venture an explanation. But in the absence of that glorious stimulant, I will instead attribute it to the beauty and inspiration of your lovely wife."

"I agree completely. Arthur, I enjoyed our breakfast and I hope we can do this more often."

"Indeed. And Jack, would you do me a favor."

"Sure, what is it?"

"Let me know what you conclude about Derek. I, too, was surprised by the circumstances of his premature demise."

"I will and may I ask you a favor also?"

"With pleasure, my good man."

"Would you call me as soon as you hear there's going to be a memorial service for Derek here in Honolulu."

"I shall ring you up immediately."

"Thank you, Arthur," Jack said as they got up from their table and walked out of the Surf Room.

Jack walked through the halls of the Royal Hawaiian, past the exhibit of silver and china that graced its dining room tables on the hotel's opening day in 1927. Once in the lobby, he looked at the window display of Panama hats and the latest patterns in Aloha shirts available at Newt's in the hotel's courtyard. He needed to talk to Jim about getting a new Panama hat. Then he decided to visit Katherine at her shop in the nearby Halekulani Hotel.

CHAPTER
TWENTY SEVEN

Mornings on Waikiki always intrigued Jack. Frenetic activity consumed every square inch of the hotel lobbies and small streets that led from the hotels to Kalakaua Avenue. Tourists were checking in and out, food was being delivered to restaurants, merchants were hawking souvenirs and tours. Taxicabs were lined up waiting for tourists who had wisely decided not to try to find their way around Honolulu in rental cars. The air held a wonderful mixture of pungent salt from the Pacific and the soft fragrance of tropical flowers from the leis that each hotel bestowed on arriving guests.

As Jack walked past the Sheraton Waikiki toward the Halekulani, he saw a group of tourists emerging from the lobby, proudly wearing what were clearly their first-ever Aloha shirts and smiled as he recalled his own first acquisition many years earlier. Then he entered the Halekulani's quiet lobby and marveled at how peaceful a retreat it was from the noise and hubbub of Waikiki.

Katherine's dress shop was strategically placed midway between the hotel's famous restaurant, La Mer, and the lobby. When Jack walked in, Katherine was leaning over the counter, reading a magazine.

"I hope that's a professional publication," Jack announced with a grin.

"It is, sort of," Katherine replied, holding up an issue of *In Style* magazine.

"Is that the current issue or one from your archives?"

"It's about six months old, but I remembered seeing a dress in an old issue that fit the description of one that Georgia just asked me to make for her, and I found it in this issue. Now, I'm trying to figure out how to do it."

"Sort of like painting from a photograph."

"Yes, except that I can't see a lot of the design detail, given the angle — you know, the structure and the seams and the sewing on the inside of the dress. And they're what make it hang and look the way it does on the outside."

"Well, I'm sure you'll figure it out."

"I will, but guess what else I found in this issue?"

"What?"

"A photograph of Derek Reynolds' wife Loretta at a Hollywood party. She's very flashy. Look!"

Jack picked up the magazine and looked at the color photograph in the center of the page, one of several that had been set in a collage of photos taken beside someone's pool at a Hollywood party. He noticed the features that Arthur had described and the thick mane of blonde hair. Loretta was an attractive woman, and Jack thought Derek must have made one hell of a case to persuade her to give up an acting career.

"Dave told me she's flying in today to pick up Derek's remains and take them back to Los Angeles for burial."

"Do you think they'll have a memorial service for Derek here in Honolulu?" Katherine asked.

"Arthur said he'd find out for me."

"How was breakfast with Arthur?"

"Great. I learned a lot about Derek and Loretta and also about the Lane's. Arthur really knows the Hollywood set."

"Well, he's been a very successful screen writer for a long time."

"Yes, and he's gotten to know a lot about their personal lives in the process."

"I can't wait to hear. Unfortunately, you'll have to wait until tonight to tell me about it over Wiki Wiki's. I have a customer coming in shortly and I've got to get some bolts of fabric out for her. Call me at noon, and maybe we can have lunch?"

"I will," Jack said, now looking intently at the collage of photographs from the Hollywood party.

"What are you staring at?" Katherine asked.

"This other photograph from the party Loretta was at," Jack said, pointing to the bottom left corner of the page. Unlike the photo of Loretta in the center of the page, this one did not have a caption identifying the people in it.

"Jack, this kind of Hollywood party collage appears in every issue. What are you getting at?"

"Look at that photo in the bottom left hand corner.

"It's hard to tell. The faces are all crowded together."

"What about on the left side of the picture, next to Loretta?"

"I don't know. If I could see more of the face, maybe I could tell."

"Can I borrow this magazine for a while?"

"Sure, just bring it home with you. I need it to make the pattern for Georgia's dress."

Jack closed the magazine, kissed his wife, and left the shop. The photograph he had asked Katherine to look at showed five people crowded around Loretta Reynolds, all of them holding drinks. The man standing next to her was wearing an ascot and holding a cigarette in his other hand.

Jack picked up the pace on his way back to the Royal Hawaiian. When he reached the lobby, he waved to Keno and asked him to get his Jeep out of the parking garage as quickly as possible.

Jack navigated the switchbacks and curves that formed the roadway to Kalakaua Avenue as fast as tourists walking in the same roadway would allow. He turned right and headed for the Diamond Head Canoe Club.

Ten minutes later, Jack jumped out of his Jeep in the parking garage and walked briskly toward the Club's entrance. As he strode through the front door, he heard Gordon Grant's booming voice growing louder as Grant walked toward him from the direction of the locker room.

"Sullivan, I've finished my morning paddle once again well before your eyes first felt the glint of the morning sun."

"Not so this morning, Grant. I've been up for hours."

"Are you feeling ill?"

"Of course not, early morning is the best time of the day to contemplate life and the challenges ahead," Jack said with the first hint of a smile.

"I couldn't agree more," Gordon replied. "It gets me ready for the tidal flow of the business world."

"Tidal flow, now there's a metaphor I haven't heard applied to the business world."

"You see, my boy, I keep telling you that you must spend more time in the Kingdom of Neptune. Tidal flow is precisely the right word for the business world — ebb and flood, currents and waves, storms and calms."

"Okay. Okay. Do they teach English in business school?"

"They teach poetry, Jack, particularly in contrast with the Old English they teach in law school."

"Touche!"

"Are you headed out?"

"Maybe."

"Don't hesitate now. I'm counting on you. You're my star pupil. I've told the entire Club that you are the future of our masters' competition."

"I won't let you down, Gordo. By the way, are you ready for the Dillingham extravaganza?"

"I am and I'm looking forward to seeing you and your lovely wife at our table."

"We'll be there. And Gordon, watch out for those riptides at work this week."

"I'll be ready for any peril that comes my way because I paid my respects to Neptune on this fine Sunday morning."

Jack walked past the lobby, through the bar, and onto the Lanai where he surveyed the Pacific. It was a good day for paddling, but he didn't have time now. Just then, he heard the voice of the man he had come to see.

"Good morning, Mr. Sullivan, are you going out paddling?" Kulani asked as he walked out on the Lanai from the bar.

"No, I'm not, Kulani. I've got a busy day ahead of me."

"Can I get you anything from the kitchen? I was just talking to the cook, and he's got some Portuguese sausage and eggs on the grill."

"It's tempting, Kulani, but I don't have time."

"Too bad. I just had a plate of them, and they were 'ono 'ono," he said, emphasizing the Hawaiian word for delicious.

"Kulani, I've got something for you to look at," Jack said as he handed Katherine's *In Style* magazine to the bartender.

"What's this?" Kulani asked.

"I want to show you a photograph and ask you if you recognize anyone in the picture."

"Which one?"

"Take a look at the photograph in the bottom left corner of the page and tell me if you recognize anyone."

Kulani picked up the magazine and studied the photograph. After thirty seconds, he put it down and looked at Jack.

"I can't say for sure, because his face is partly blocked by the woman standing next to him. But the guy on the left looks a little like the driver of the car that ran me off the road."

"How can you say that if you can't see most of his face?"

"Because he has one of those neck scarves on like men wore in old movies and the collar of his shirt is turned up and he has that same look, the one I saw in the car that night, looking over at me."

"How about his hair?"

"I can't tell because I really didn't see it. The driver had a hat on, and it was dark."

"Is there anything else about him that you recognize from that night?"

"No, Mr. Sullivan, but there is one other thing."

"What's that?"

"I have a feeling I've seen this guy somewhere else. I just don't know where."

"Have you seen him here in Honolulu?"

"Mr. Sullivan, I've never been anywhere but Oahu my whole life. If I saw him, it was here."

"Did you see him here at the Club?"

"I don't know. I can't remember. I work part-time at hotels when there are big conventions, and I see a lot of people."

"But you think you've seen this guy someplace in Honolulu?"

"I do."

"When do you think you saw him?"

"That look. That shirt. Even the way he holds a cigarette. I must have seen him recently to remember it all. I know I've seen a guy who looks like that, and it wasn't too long ago."

"Keep thinking about it, will you, Kulani, and let me know if it comes back to you."

"I will, Mr. Sullivan."

Jack called Katherine and confirmed that they would meet for lunch on the lanai at the Halekulani, then called Dave McNeil and said he needed to see him as soon as possible. Dave told him to come to Police Headquarters at one-thirty.

CHAPTER
TWENTY EIGHT

Jack met Katherine at Orchids, the restaurant on the lanai of the Halekulani, at eleven-thirty, and Katherine immediately knew that her husband was excited about something.

"What happened after you left my shop, hubby?" Katherine asked.

"I went to the Club."

"And?"

"I talked to Gordon Grant."

"And?"

"I talked to Kulani."

"Jack, don't make me depose you!"

"I won't. I just wanted to see how quickly you'd figure it out."

"What?"

"This," Jack said as he held up the magazine Katherine had given him that morning. "It may be the key that unlocks the mystery to Derek Reynolds' death."

"How?"

"Take a look at that photograph of Loretta Reynolds at the party."

"I already saw it."

"I showed this picture to Kulani at the Club, and he thinks the guy standing next to Loretta looks like the person who ran him off the road the night after the cast party."

"Why does he think that?"

"The ascot, which he described to the police as the kind of scarf men wore in old movies. The turned-up collar. The cigarette. The look."

"He remembers all that?"

"Not all of it from the incident on the beach road out at Kailua. Some of it comes from seeing someone somewhere else on Oahu who looks like this guy."

"Where on Oahu? For heaven's sake, Jack, Arthur Fairbanks wears an ascot!"

"So does George Lane, as I learned when I had lunch at the Lane's. But, to get back to your question, there can't be too many places where Kulani has seen this guy or someone who looks like him. Kulani works at the Club most nights and at hotels when there are conventions."

"Has he seen this person recently?"

"He thinks so."

"So why do you think this photograph may be the key to the mystery?"

"Because the guy in this photograph was at the same Hollywood party as Derek Reynolds' wife Loretta."

"I'm not following you."

"Loretta was very unhappy about Derek's philandering in general and in particular with Hypatia."

"Keep going."

"In response, she was dating young actors and going to Hollywood parties with them."

"Why does that matter?"

"Because she reviewed all of the screenplays that Derek considered."

"How sure are you of that?"

"Both Bob Street and Arthur Fairbanks told me."

"And that's important because …?"

"Because one screenplay she recently reviewed was a classic mystery along the lines of Alfred Hitchcock, in which the victim was poisoned. Right here in Hawaii."

"And the poison was 'Akia!"

"You got it!"

"Jack, that's fine as far as it goes. But we know that Loretta wasn't at the party where Derek was poisoned."

"No, she wasn't, but maybe the guy in this photograph was."

"So you think they're dating. But why would she murder her husband or, should I say, have him murdered? She's hardly the only Hollywood wife whose husband is cheating on her, and there hasn't exactly been a rash of Hollywood men murdered lately."

"I sense from talking with Arthur that Derek gave Loretta plenty of reasons to be angry with him, not the least of which were the loss of her career and damage to her dignity. His affair with Hypatia may have been the last straw."

"Why this particular affair?" Katherine asked.

"Maybe she thought Derek would actually leave her this time," Jack surmised. "From all accounts, he was over the edge with Hypatia."

"I thought you told me that Derek gave lots of people plenty of reasons to dislike him, including the Lane's."

"That's true. In fact, coincidentally, the Lane's have a similar motive and the means to do him in, and they absolutely had the opportunity because they were at the cast party."

"How could they have done it?"

"They know all about Hawaiian plants, customs and rituals. And they grow 'Akia in their garden."

"The poisonous kind?"

"I don't know, but there was an empty patch of freshly turned soil next to one of their 'Akia shrubs."

"Do you think they did it?"

"I don't know. I do know they had a disastrous career experience with Derek earlier in their lives and a very negative reaction when they saw him in The Poinciana Hotel on the Saturday before the cast party. Hell, they checked out the next morning when they were planning to stay for five days. And when I had lunch at their place, they didn't even mention their very recent trip to the Poinciana, even though they did tell me they visit the Big Island frequently."

"Anyone else?"

"Yes, sweet one. Guess who else knows all about Hawaiian plants and flowers?"

"Who?"

"Jennifer Adams."

"Of course, she buys tropical plants and flowers from that florist over in Kailua."

"Yes, and he is very impressed with the deep interest she has shown in all kinds of Hawaiian plants, which extends to taking field trips whenever she comes to Oahu."

"And the field where you found the poisonous 'Akia is not far from that flower shop, is it?"

"No."

"And she was at the party too."

"Yes, and she had a loud argument with Derek the preceding Saturday evening at the Poinciana."

"Which the Lane's observed without being seen."

"Exactly."

"And her motive?"

"Jennifer vehemently dislikes Derek because of the way he treats her sister. Arthur told me that Jennifer believes Derek physically abused Hypatia."

"Did he?"

"I don't know, but Jennifer thinks so."

"So, what are you going to do next?"

"I'm going to lay out my evidence to Dave McNeil at one- thirty."

"Who gets your vote?"

"Until I nail down the mystery man in that photo, I can't really connect anything to Loretta or to him. And I can't ignore the motives, means and opportunities that both of the Lane's and Jennifer Adams had."

"So you're reserving judgment until you develop more evidence?"

"Spoken like the insightful and careful lawyer you are, my dear."

"Oh please!"

"Yes, expressed in very lawyerly terms. You can take the girl out of the law firm but ..."

"Oh, Jack," Katherine said laughing.

Realizing that they had not yet ordered lunch, Jack waved to the maitre'd, who smiled and dispatched a waitress to their table.

"I thought you'd never ask, Jack."

"I'm sorry, Katherine. I just got wound up and couldn't stop."

"That's all right. I'm proud of you and I have a feeling that you're close. But no more talk about Derek until we finish our lunch."

Katherine enjoyed an oriental chicken salad, and Jack a papaya mango salad, and they both drank glasses of pineapple iced tea. The turquoise Pacific filled their view from the lanai, and only a row of yellow hibiscus flowers, a sliver of grass, and a low green hedge of naupaka shrubs separated their table from the sea.

"What a spot! It's like looking through a picture window," Jack said, sipping the sweet tea.

"Yes, it's just perfect."

"So what do you think? Shall I go for it?"

"Absolutely. I doubt that the police have analyzed this case as well as you have."

"You know, I don't think they have, at least not yet. I think I've got something here."

"I do too. I'll pick up the check, Jack. You get over to see Dave.

"Thanks, baby," Jack said as he leaned over the table to kiss his wife. "I'll call you when I leave Dave's office."

"Good luck. But I do have one more question, Jack."

"Shoot."

"What's the connection between the guy in this photo and Derek? Is it merely that you think he may be dating Loretta?"

"Elementary, my dear wife. Yes, I think he may be dating her but, more importantly, the guy in the photograph with Loretta is wearing an ascot and a shirt with a turned-up collar, just like the driver of the car that Kulani described to the police. And he's probably an actor if he's in that picture."

"But what's the connection with Kulani?"

"Maybe he was at the cast party and suspected that Kulani saw him, maybe even saw him do something suspicious. If so, Kulani could bring him to the attention of the police. So why not eliminate the bartender, the one person who had a view of all the people at the party and the one person who could have seen him slip poison into a drink that was bound for Derek Reynolds?"

"I see. But what's his motive?"

"I don't know, but that photograph suggests he's got some kind of relationship with Derek's wife. And there's one other thing."

"What?"

"The guy smokes."

"And you found a Camel under the 'Akia bush out in Kailua."

"Yep, and Dave McNeil found one in the ashtray of the Ford Taurus that Reynolds' production company rented, the one that ran Kulani off the road in Kailua."

"Does anybody else in this group you've assembled smoke Camels?"

"I didn't see any ashtrays at the Lanes' house, but George Lane's right hand is covered with tobacco stains. Unfortunately, I didn't see what kind of cigarette he smokes. But his house is not far from Kailua."

"I doubt that he'd steal a car from Reynolds' production company, Jack."

"I agree, but he could have been careless and left a cigarette butt on the field out in Kailua."

"But he would have gone there only if the 'Akia that grows in their garden is the non-poisonous kind and he had to go out there to get the high test stuff."

"Or if they didn't have enough of the strong stuff in their garden to produce sufficient poison."

"Jack, you don't think they'd use 'Akia from their own garden, do you? That would be too obvious and incriminating."

"I would agree with you, Katherine, except for that empty patch of freshly turned soil I saw next to their 'Akia bushes. And they'd sure know where to get the high-test variety because they know everything there is to know about Hawaiian plants. Plus, George was out at a nursery yesterday afternoon when I arrived at the Lane's for lunch, buying a new shrub, probably to cover that empty patch of soil next to the 'Akia bush."

"One more question, Jack. Does Jennifer smoke Camels?"

Smiling, Jack replied, "I don't even know if she smokes cigarettes, but I'd like to find out."

CHAPTER
TWENTY NINE

Jack arrived at Police Headquarters in downtown Honolulu at one-fifteen and was standing outside Dave McNeil's door two minutes later.

"Come on in, Jack", Dave said while holding his hand over the phone. "I'm just finishing a call. Grab some of Honolulu's finest supermarket coffee. It's only been brewing since seven this morning."

Jack smiled and passed up the opportunity to test the dark and ever-thickening liquid from Dave's electric drip coffee maker. Dave nodded his head as he said 'yes' into the phone twice before hanging up.

"That was Derek Reynolds' executive vice president, who accompanied Mrs. Reynolds to Honolulu. They've arrived at their hotel, the Oriental, and will be attending a memorial service there for Derek early this evening. It looks like I don't have much time to gather my troops for an interview with her."

"Is this the first time you've had an opportunity to talk to Mrs. Reynolds?"

"I spoke with her on the phone early Tuesday morning but she was a bit upset and not in a frame of mind to talk to me or anyone else from the Police Department."

"And, of course, you didn't know then what you know now."

"No, we didn't. And by that look on your face and the tone of your voice, you're about to tell me more that I don't know."

"I am."

Jack summarized everything he had learned during the past twenty-four hours about Jennifer's interest in Hawaiian plants, the Lanes' gardens, Derek's philandering, Loretta's response, the two screenplays set in Hawaii, the use of 'Akia as a poison in one of the screenplays, and the man in the Hollywood party photograph with Loretta. Dave listened attentively and asked to see the *In Style* magazine.

"I see what you mean about this guy in the photograph. He does fit the description Kulani gave us of the driver of the car that ran him off the road. And it does look like he's a smoker."

"He probably also knows Loretta Reynolds, Dave."

"The question, Jack, is how well he knows her. She seems quite unlike someone who would direct the murder of her husband."

"How's your crime scene search team coming with their analysis of the Ford Taurus? Have they found any fingerprints they can identify?"

"They were able to lift several discrete sets of prints, Jack, but they haven't been able to identify all of the hands that belong to them. Some were obviously left by employees of the car rental company and those we have identified. Others we simply haven't been able to match with any prints in the national data base."

"How about the cigarette butts? Is there enough DNA on them to identify the smoker?"

"Yes, but as I thought, we don't have any DNA characteristics in the national data base that match the DNA we got from the cigarette butts. So we're in the same boat that we are with the fingerprints we lifted from the Taurus."

"I guess what you need is a suspect whose fingerprints you can compare with the prints from the car and who can give you some saliva to compare with what you've got on the cigarette butts."

"That would do it, Jack. And with all due respect for the fine work you've done to date, I'm not sure we've got a case right now against any of the suspects you've identified."

"I agree, but I've got an idea."

"Shoot."

"I'm going to do a little prospecting, for suspects rather than gold."

"I don't want you putting yourself in harm's way, old buddy. That's my job. That's why I get paid the big bucks."

"I hear you. The only harm that can come my way is the threat of a defamation suit, and I know how to avoid that."

"What are you thinking?"

"I'm going to attend the memorial service at the Oriental, and I'd like you to have a few of Honolulu's finest there, in plain clothes of course, but ready to act if I give you what I think I'll be able to."

"Jack, this isn't a television series. If there's a murderer at this service, he may decide that you're an inconvenience he can do without."

"Or she. Or he and she."

"Yes, depending upon which of your suspects gets the most agitated with your accusation."

"Oh, I'm not going to accuse anyone. I'm just going to have a few conversations."

"And then?"

"We're going to honor the memory of Derek Reynolds and see what happens."

"Okay. I'll go with you on this one, because of your instincts as much as your evidence. And I'll have some officers stationed inside and outside the Oriental. We'll just characterize it as security to keep the public from interfering and making a spectacle of the memorial service."

"Excellent."

"Jack, do you mind my asking what the hell kind of conversations you're going to have with these people?"

"They're going to be very social, Dave. That's the kind of guy I am."

"Do you plan to record them?"

"No, I don't think that will be necessary. But I would ask you to have a crime scene lab technician remain on duty tonight. I may have some work for him."

"Okay."

"And one other thing, Dave. I know you'll do this, but would you be sure to explore this screenplay issue with Mrs. Reynolds, if you can do it without jeopardizing the rest of your investigation?"

"I will. I'm as curious as you are to see her reaction to the news that her husband died of acute poisoning from an 'Akia plant."

"That will tell us a lot, Dave."

"That it will. Now, I've got to organize my troops for that interview. I'll see you at five-thirty at the Oriental."

"I'll be there."

Jack left Police Headquarters at two-thirty for the Diamond Head Canoe Club. Along the way, he called Katherine, told her he would be attending the memorial service for Derek, and that he needed her magazine a little longer. He also left a voicemail message for Arthur, letting him know the exact time and place of the service. Jack had decided that Gordon Grant was right. He needed some time with Neptune to clear his head and prepare for the unusual Sunday evening that lay ahead. As Jack drove toward Kalakaua Avenue, his cell phone rang and a familiar voice greeted him when he answered his phone.

"Jack, this is Maile."

"Maile, how are you? Have I forgotten to return a book to the Bishop Museum's library on time?"

"No," Maile said laughing.

"Thank God. I was afraid the library police would be knocking on my door."

"No, Jack, you're one of the most trustworthy users of our resources. But I am calling you about your research, sort of."

"What do you mean?"

"Do you remember when you asked me about the procedures for logging visitors in and out of the library?"

"Yes."

"Well, I checked, and we do have fairly strict procedures for using the library."

"Good. That protects the Museum."

"There's just one problem, Jack."

"What's that?"

"While we require everyone to log in, it seems that someone logged in recently and wrote a name that is illegible. We're not sure who it is."

"Are any books missing?"

"No, but there is something I thought you should know."

"What's that?"

"I checked with the librarian who was on duty at the desk those days, and she remembered a man asking where the books on Hawaiian plants and traditions were located, just like you did. So I thought you'd want to know that someone else was recently interested in these subjects. I just had a feeling it was important to you."

"It is, Maile. Does the librarian remember what the man looked like?"

"I didn't ask her, Jack. I'm sorry."

"That's all right. Maybe I'll drop by and talk to her."

"She'll be at the library tomorrow morning. And, by the way, Papa David called me and wanted your phone number so I gave it to him. I hope you don't mind."

"Of course not, when did he call?"

"Just before I called you, so I better hang up. He may be trying to reach you."

"Okay, Maile. Thanks for calling."

Just as Jack reached the Diamond Head Canoe Club, his cell phone rang again.

"Jack, this is Papa David."

"Good afternoon sir, how are you?"

"I'm fine, Jack, and I have some information for you that may be important."

"What is it?"

"I had lunch today with another practitioner of herbal medicine, and we got talking about the recent spate of poisonings from the Angel's Trumpet flower and Oleander, and he told me the strangest story."

"I think I know what's coming. Go ahead."

"Recently, he received a telephone call from a man who wanted to come in to see him but first wanted to know what herbal medicine could do for his ailment, which he described as arthritis. And in the course of discussing his condition with my colleague, he began to talk about plants that were used in ancient Hawaiian rituals, and one he brought up was 'Akia. My colleague was quite surprised, because 'Akia is not a plant that herbal medicine professionals would use to treat any medical condition, much less arthritis."

"Did he ask where he could find 'Akia."

"Yes, and my colleague told him to be careful not to use the poisonous kind for any purpose."

"Did your colleague also tell him where the poisonous kind grows, so that he could avoid contact with it?"

"He did. He told him about the field that you and I visited."

"Would I be presumptuous, Papa David, if I concluded that this caller never actually visited your colleague for treatment?"

"Jack, he never heard from the man again."

"I'm not surprised. Thank you, Papa David. That is very helpful."

CHAPTER THIRTY

The Pacific surf was barely breaking on the reef when Jack cruised
through its narrow opening on his outrigger canoe. As soon as
he cleared the reef, he pressed the right foot pedal and turned the
boat toward the Waikiki hotels. He took long and smooth strokes
with the black carbon fiber paddle that propelled the white hull
through the blue water swiftly enough to throw an aquamarine
bow wave forward and leave a gurgling white wake behind.

Jack increased the rate of his strokes and began to plan the
conversations he would have at the memorial service for Derek
Reynolds. As he had done in preparation for so many trials, Jack
catalogued those he would have conversations with, then settled
on the substance of each conversation, and finally determined
the order in which he would have those conversations. He was
confident that he would have enough information when he finished to convince Dave.

The Oriental was only ten minutes from the Diamond Head
Canoe Club, but Jack knew he could not take any chance that
he would be late. He paddled hard for fifteen minutes, until he
was just past the Natatorium, then turned his canoe back toward
the jetty that marked one end of the Club's beach. The Pacific
remained calm this Sunday afternoon and, fifteen minutes later,
Jack was passing through the opening in the reef, riding the crest
of a gentle wave that carried him to the beach.

After a quick shower, Jack stopped in to see the Club manager, Noa Watson, and the two of them walked to the bar to talk to Kulani.

"Kulani, I think I know where we can find the guy who ran you off the road," Jack said, "but I need your help to tell me whether or not you see him when I take you where I think he might be."

"What do you want me to do?"

"Our distinguished Club Manager has graciously agreed to take over the bar for a couple of hours while you and I go on a little expedition where we just might spot the bird that tried to do you in."

Kulani looked at Noa, who nodded his assent and broke into a broad grin.

"Kulani, you could perform no higher service for the Club than to help identify the criminal who tried to run Honolulu's best bartender off the road."

"Thank you, Noa. I will do my best."

Jack thanked Noa for his indulgence and left the Club with Kulani at his side.

"What do you want me to do, Mr. Sullivan?" Kulani asked as the Jeep wound its way along Diamond Head Road, around the base of the Diamond Head crater, toward the Oriental Hotel.

"I want you to stay with the car in front of the hotel until I come to get you. Then I want you to come into the hotel with me and tell me if you see the guy who ran you off the road."

Jack reached the semi-circular driveway in front of the Oriental Hotel ten minutes later and noticed two very plain white sedans parked at the edge of the circle. Shaking his head and laughing quietly to himself, Jack recalled his days as a prosecutor and images of the markedly bland sedans that metropolitan police departments regularly employ as "unmarked" police cars. As he approached the hotel's entrance, Jack also noticed four uniformed members of the Honolulu Police Department stand-ing beside two clearly marked police cruisers. Dave had covered the hotel with his troops just as Jack had asked, but Dave was nowhere to be seen.

The Oriental Hotel was very elegant. Jack thought it had a New York feel about it. He was not surprised that many cast members and Derek Reynolds, as well as other executives of his production company, had chosen the Oriental as their residence for the duration of filming on Oahu. As the many photographs of movie stars on its lobby wall attested, the Oriental was a favorite of the Hollywood set.

The hotel's ballrooms were located one level below the lobby, and Jack could hear the low buzz of muffled conversations as soon as he reached the staircase that led down to the Wailae Room. The only security at its entrance was an attractive public relations representative who smiled at everyone who entered the room.

The Wailae Room's rear wall was composed of black volca-nic rock. Heavy glass chandeliers surrounded by green metal-lic maile leaves hung from recessed squares in the ceiling. A mahogany bar occupied the right rear corner of the room, and an elevated stage with a podium was on the left side of the room. The chandeliers cast a warm glow on the turquoise and brown carpet below.

Jack estimated that there were about a hundred and fifty people in the room, most of whom he did not recognize and thus categorized as members of the cast and employees of the produc-tion company. Gordon Grant was there, representing the Club. The Mayor of Honolulu was standing with the President of the Hawaii Chamber of Commerce. Arthur Fairbanks was engaged in animated conversation with the Lane's. And Hypatia and Jennifer Adams were standing alone in a corner of the room. As soon as Gordon saw Jack, he made a beeline for him.

"Man, am I glad to see you," Gordon said with obvious relief. I was hoping you'd be here. I didn't want to go through this without my lawyer."

"Can I bill you for this representation?"

"Absolutely. You can charge me your full east coast rate too. Just don't leave early or wander off where I can't grab you."

"Don't worry, Gordo. Nobody's going to accuse the Club of anything."

"How can you be so sure?"

"I'm sure on this one. So just relax and enjoy the show. I'll be back later."

Jack walked toward Hypatia and Jennifer and, as he approached, Hypatia greeted him.

"Jack, we had such a wonderful visit with Katherine. Please tell her how much we love her things and can't wait to have her design dresses for us. We'll be sure to stop by again before we leave Honolulu."

"Thank you, Hypatia. I'll do that, and I know she'll be thrilled. By the way, she loved the plants and flowers you sent, Jennifer. They really improved the decor. I'm afraid that, for all of her other artistic talents, my wife's thumb is not green."

"Oh, Jennifer knows all about tropical plants and flowers and can grow anything," Hypatia said.

"Thanks again, Jennifer. I'm sure you'll get a note from Katherine if she has your address."

"I gave her one of my cards, Jack, and I hope she visits my flower shop in L.A. some day. In fact, I wish I were there today. Anywhere but here."

"Well, these memorials are always difficult. I know what you mean."

"No, you don't know what I mean. This guy was a real shit. I can't believe I'm showing respect for him by being here. Actually, I can't figure out why anyone is here."

"Jennifer, that's enough," Hypatia said. "We've been through this three times today."

"Why are you here? He didn't do anything for you other than stalk you, push you around, and tell everyone in Hollywood lies about you and him."

"Jack, I'm sorry, but Jennifer has a rather negative view of Derek that I asked her to contain during this service."

"Look around, Jack," Jennifer interjected. "Do you see a wet eye in the house? I don't think so. And you won't find one anywhere in Hollywood either. In fact, I'll be surprised if his wife can muster a tear for the bastard."

"Jennifer, please."

"I think I better leave you two alone to work this one out," Jack said.

"I'm sorry, Jack," said Hypatia with a frown clearly aimed at her sister.

"Don't think twice about it. I'll tell Katherine you'll stop by to see her before you go back to California."

"Please do and tell her I'll bring a better-behaved little sister when I come by."

Jack bid the Adams sisters adieu and put Jennifer at the bottom of his list of suspects. She may know a lot about Hawaiian plants and she probably knows about 'Akia, he thought, but it was unlikely that someone who was so public with her contempt and disdain for Derek Reynolds would do him in, even though she undoubtedly enjoyed every aspect of his demise.

Jack next turned his attention to Sidney and George Lane, who were still talking with Arthur Fairbanks.

"Jack, I got your message. Thanks for calling me."

"I'm glad I reached you in time, Arthur."

"Hello, Sidney. Hello, George."

"Jack, how wonderful it is to see you again," Sidney said. "We so loved showing you our garden."

"The pleasure was all mine, Sidney. George, I must tell you, the variety of plants you have out there would impress the botanists who sailed with Captain Cook."

"And Jack would know that, George," Arthur interjected proudly. "He's read everything about Captain Cook's voyages to the Pacific."

"Really, Jack. And I thought you were just a lawyer turned coffee farmer," George said, an edge of condescension in his voice.

"Well, as I mentioned at lunch, I'm trying to learn as much as I can about Hawaii's history and that inevitably drew me to Captain Cook."

"That must have required a great deal of reading," George observed. "Where did you do your research, Jack?"

"At the Bishop Museum. I'm sure you've been there more than a few times."

"Yes, I spent quite a bit of time there myself when we were selecting plants and flowers for our garden."

"Well, it's an extraordinary resource, sort of like your library."

"Yes", George replied, "In fact, I tried to acquire as many of the old horticultural and botanical books as I could so I wouldn't have to drive out to the Bishop Museum every time I wanted to plant another part of our garden."

"I'm sure you've got every book that matters."

"No, there are some that have been out of print for a long time and others are only available at the Bishop. Luckily, the Bishop Museum seems to have them all, even those that would be impossible to find, except at estate sales."

"Have you been there recently?" Jack asked.

Jack couldn't be certain, but George appeared to be startled by the question.

Just then, there was a stir at the entrance to the Wailae Room, and a striking woman with thick blonde hair strode into the room, led by a dark-suited man who was obviously from the business side of Derek Reynolds' operation. They walked up three steps to the stage and stood at the podium. The crowd grew silent as the executive vice-president of Reynolds Productions stood at the microphone.

"Ladies and Gentlemen, thank you for coming to honor our colleague and friend, Derek Reynolds. I know we all miss him terribly and I know you are all wondering what will happen to you and to our production here in Hawaii. I have talked with Mrs. Reynolds about it, and she would like to speak to you directly."

As Loretta Reynolds walked to the microphone, Jack was once again surprised that Derek could have persuaded her to give up an acting career. She was tall with high cheekbones and an athletic build that was evident in spite of her plain black dress. She radiated a presence that only the most formidable movie stars project, and those present were obviously mesmerized at the sight of her.

"Thank you for coming here this evening. My husband would have been honored to see all of you remembering him. It gives me great comfort to know that you all cared so much for him. And so I have decided that the best memorial we can give Derek is to continue the production here in Hawaii and make this the best movie he ever produced. Thank you very much, and now I think we should all enjoy our favorite refreshments at the kind of party that Derek would have enjoyed."

The applause quickly moved beyond a dignified response to a very enthusiastic clapping and then to outright cheers. Jack was not surprised at the reaction. The members of the cast and the employees of the production company weren't there because they loved Derek Reynolds. They were there because they needed work, and Loretta Reynolds knew it. Jennifer was right, Jack mused; there wasn't a wet eye in the house, including those at the podium.

Out of the corner of his eye, Jack saw Dave McNeil standing just outside the entrance to the room where he, too, had been listening to Loretta's remarks. When he saw Jack looking in his direction, he nodded imperceptibly. Dave was ready for Jack's signal.

Loretta stepped down from the podium and began to work the crowd. She was accompanied by Derek's executive vice-president every step of the way, leading Jack to conclude that Loretta had been a very important component of the business side of Reynolds Productions. Jack watched as Loretta moved among the cast members and the production company employees. She thanked each member individually for coming and urged each to stay with the production and complete Derek's final movie. The employees of Reynolds Productions could not have been more responsive to her. They lined up to greet her and convey their condolences just as the bar opened with great fanfare at the other end of the room and waiters with trays of hors d'oeuvres and white wine began circulating. A memorial service, Hollywood style, Jack thought.

As Jack watched Loretta, he was impressed with the composure she maintained as she spoke to each person. She would extend her right hand, nod her head, say a few words in a quiet tone, and then move on to the next member of the cast or production team until she encountered a young man who was obviously a member of the cast. Dressed in a white linen sport coat and pink polo shirt with yellow pleated trousers, he looked as if he had just been posing for an ad in a fashion magazine. Loretta barely acknowledged his presence and quickly moved beyond him to the next member of the cast.

Jack had the overwhelming sense that he had seen this man before. Studying him, he recognized a few of the features he had seen in the magazine photograph of the Hollywood party that Loretta had attended. When the man headed for the bar in the back of the room, Jack decided to join him. They reached the bar at the same time, but the bartender was already flooded with orders and Jack turned toward the young man.

"Could you grab me one of those short glasses on the table over to your right? I hate to drink cocktails out of highball glasses when I'm having my liquor on the rocks. And I'm going to pour this one myself to help the bartender out."

"Sure", the young man replied as he took a short glass from the table on his right and placed it on the bar in front of Jack.

"This is a tough occasion," Jack said.

"Yes, it is," the man replied curtly. "Are you associated with the production company?"

"No. I'm a local. I'm a member of the Canoe Club and wanted to pay my respects to Mr. Reynolds, who did so much for Hawaii by filming his movie here on Oahu. Are you with the production company?"

"I'm a member of the cast."

"Really?" What's your name, so I'll be able to say I met you when the movie comes out."

"Lance Forbes."

"Lance, I'm Jack Sullivan. It's a pleasure to meet you."

"Nice to meet you, Mr. Sullivan."

"Please, call me Jack. I came out here to get away from stuffiness. I think of Mr. Sullivan as my father."

As Lance tried to get the bartender's attention, Jack noticed a bulge in the pocket of his sport coat. It was rectangular but not large enough to be a wallet.

"Say Lance, I forgot my cigarettes. You don't by any chance smoke, do you?"

"You're in luck, Jack," Lance said as he pulled a pack of Camels out of his sport coat pocket and offered Jack one.

"I am in luck. Not only a cigarette but a real cigarette."

"The only kind I've smoked since I was ten," Lance said as he turned away from Jack toward the bartender.

"Lance, you're a true American. Thanks for the cigarette and good luck with this movie. I'll look for you in the credits," Jack said as he poured Scotch into the glass, picked it up by the bottom, and walked away from the bar toward the entrance to the room where Dave was standing.

"Stay right here and don't say anything to Kulani or me when we walk back through here in a minute," Jack said under his breath as he passed Dave.

Jack walked briskly to his Jeep in front of the hotel and waved to Kulani, who promptly jumped out of the front passenger seat. Jack continued walking to the car, emptied the Scotch on the lawn, and then wrapped the short cocktail glass he had carried from the bar in a beach towel that lay on the back seat.

"Kulani, I want you to walk into the Wailae Room behind me. Don't act as if we know each other and don't say a word to Dave McNeil, who is standing by the door. When you get into the room, there are going to be a lot of people. Look over toward the bar in the back of the room and see if you recognize anyone. If you do, just walk back out through the door and I'll meet you there."

Jack walked into the lobby, turned to see that Kulani was not following too closely, and walked down the steps to the Wailae Room. He made eye contact with Dave McNeil, who nodded slightly to let Jack know that he saw Kulani coming. When Jack entered the room, his eyes flashed to the bar where, as he expected, Lance Forbes was still standing, smoking and talking to other members of the cast. Jack stood aside and watched Kulani enter the room, walk past him, stop, and then direct his gaze to the back of the room where the bar was located. Kulani's brow furrowed. His eyes narrowed in a squint, and he walked farther through the crowd, obviously to get a closer look. To Jack, it seemed like an eternity had passed when, suddenly, Kulani turned on his heel and walked out of the room. Jack waited a discreet moment, checked to see whether Lance had noticed Kulani, and then followed him out of the room.

"That's him!" Kulani proclaimed.

"Who?" Jack asked as Dave McNeil joined them.

"The guy who ran me off the road."

"Which guy was it?"

"The guy in the white coat and the pink shirt, smoking a cigarette by the bar. I'd know that look anywhere and now I know where I've seen him before."

"Where?"

"At the bar in the Club on Monday night at the cast party. He sat there most of the evening with his back to me, but every once in a while I saw his face because, with the crowd, I had to hand him drinks to pass to waitresses."

"Are you sure?" Dave asked.

"I'm positive."

"Okay, Kulani, why don't you meet me back at the Jeep. Dave and I will take care of things here."

"Give me two minutes with that guy. That's all I need."

"I know, but we've got something better in store for him that you'll enjoy even more," Jack said.

"Okay. I'll see you at the Jeep."

Jack turned to Dave as Kulani walked away.

"I've got a short cocktail glass with this guy's fingerprints on it in the back seat of my Jeep. His name is Lance Forbes, and he's a member of the cast. If you give me about two minutes, I'll get you a Camel cigarette butt this guy just smoked. Oh, and by the way, one of the librarians at the Bishop Museum told me that some guy logged in recently, asking to look at books on Hawaiian plants and customs. And a guy called one of Papa David's fellow practitioners and asked him whether 'Akia was a remedy for arthritis. After he told the guy it wouldn't help his arthritis, he also told him to be careful not to come into contact with the

'Akia that grows out in the field near Kailua, where I found the high-test stuff, because it was poisonous."

With that, Jack walked back into the Wailae Room to the bar where Lance was still holding court with several other members of the cast. Beside him on the table was an ashtray containing several Camel cigarette butts. No one else was smoking.

"I couldn't hit you up for another one of those Camels could I, Lance?"

"Sure, Jack. These guys aren't man enough to smoke them," Lance said as he reached into his pocket for the pack of cigarettes. At the same time, Jack moved his long arm over the table and let his right hand dangle above the ashtray. When he was sure no one was looking, he reached in and snared a still- moist cigarette butt, enveloping it in his fist.

"Thank you, Lance," Jack said, accepting another Camel with his left hand. "And good luck again."

Jack walked through the increasingly loud and intoxicated crowd and met Dave at his post outside the Wailae Room.

"Have you by any chance got a plastic evidence bag in your pocket? I've got some evidence for you that I'd like to get out of my possession and into yours."

"It just so happens, Detective Sullivan, that I brought several evidence bags along for the evening."

"Here is a still-wet Camel cigarette butt that I just retrieved from the ashtray on the table next to Lance Forbes, who was the only person in that group smoking, and who earlier gave me this - still unsmoked – Camel cigarette from the pack he took out of his sport coat pocket. He gave me this second unsmoked Camel a moment ago."

"I like a man who respects the integrity of the chain of custody of evidence."

"So do I, Dave, so let's get to my fingerprint evidence before someone spoils it."

Jack took Dave to his Jeep, where Kulani was standing, reached into the back seat, and dropped the short cocktail glass into another plastic evidence bag that Dave held open.

"I want to enter into another wager with you, Dave."

"What's this one?"

"When your crime scene lab technicians compare the fingerprints on this glass to some of the prints they lifted from the Ford Taurus, they'll find a match. And when your DNA guys compare the saliva from the Camel I just took from the ashtray with the saliva from the Camel that I found under the bush out in the field at Kailua, and with the saliva from the Camel your guys found in the ashtray of the Ford Taurus, they will conclude that they all came from the same person, namely, Lance Forbes.

"And when the librarian at the Bishop Museum gets a look at Lance Forbes in a lineup, I bet she'll say he's the man who recently consulted books on Hawaiian plants and culture. And when Papa David's fellow herbal medicine practitioner hears Lance Forbes' voice, I bet he'll identify it as the person who called him and asked whether 'Akia could be used as a treatment for arthritis."

"I wouldn't be a bit surprised," Dave said with a smile.

"Now why, my good man, would you not be surprised if all this were to occur?"

"Because I had a very productive conversation with Mrs. Reynolds earlier this evening. And, by the way, she's a very impressive lady."

"Yes, and I assume you learned that she has been seeing one Lance Forbes?"

"As a matter of fact, I did. But I also asked some other questions, including the ones you specifically asked me to pose to her about the screenplay for the movie where the victim was poisoned with 'Akia."

"And she admitted that she'd read it, right?"

"She did. She told me that she regularly reviewed all of the screenplays that were submitted to Derek and that he consulted her on every choice he made. And he usually went with her recommendation, except on this one, which made Loretta really mad. She knew Derek rejected it solely because it didn't have a role that would showcase Hypatia."

"Did she come right out and tell you that or did you have to pull it out of her?"

"She was quite forthcoming. So forthcoming that she told me right off the bat who else reviewed that screenplay after she read it and who agreed with her assessment."

"Who was that?"

"The young actor she was dating in retaliation for Derek pursuing Hypatia Adams. Lance Forbes."

"That's it, Dave. You've got it. I mean you got him."

"We got him, Jack. And, by the way, there's more. You want some motive?"

"I do."

"Loretta was furious when Derek made a public spectacle of his pursuit of Hypatia. And yet she had lived through his philandering before, so it wasn't completely new to her. She was always comforted by the fact that she was an intellectual as well as financial partner in Derek's business. He really did rely on her judgment before he chose screenplays, and she never picked a bad one. But when Derek rejected the Hitchcock-type mystery she had recommended and selected the B-rate movie they're filming here, she flipped out and felt she was losing the last vestige of her marriage that meant anything to her. She was a mess according to her own description."

"So where does Lance Forbes come into the picture? No pun intended."

"Well said, Jack. You always come up with just the right words."

"Spare me the bullshit, Dave."

"Here's why I won't wager with you. She asked Lance to review the Hitchcock-type screenplay with 'Akia in it as well as the screenplay for the movie they're filming out here to get a second opinion. She wanted to make sure she wasn't off base. That's how conscientious she is, and that's how much she cared about Derek's career."

"So what did Lance say?"

"Not only did Lance agree with her that the Hitchcock alternative was clearly better, he tried to persuade her to leave Derek and marry him."

"What was her response to that?"

"She rejected it out of hand and told him she'd never leave Derek. Loretta thinks Lance convinced himself that she could get big movie parts for him if they were married. And that he wouldn't mind sharing her big bank account either."

"Big movie parts and a big bank account, I assume, that he couldn't get on his own. So he went off, with a head start because he'd read the screenplay that Derek selected and then got a minor role in the movie. And he knew about the poisonous Hawaiian plant from the other screenplay that Loretta had also given him to read. Poor old Derek's days were numbered at that point," Jack said, shaking his head.

"To use one of your favorite words, Jack, Bingo! The evidence you've turned up will prove, I'm sure, that Lance then decided to take matters into his own hands and remove the obstacle to his aspirations, namely Derek Reynolds."

"So when are you going to arrest him, Dave?"

"Right now, based on Kulani's identification of him as the guy who ran him off the road. We've got the tread marks; we'll do the comparison of his fingerprints from the cocktail glass with those on the Taurus tonight; and we should have the DNA from his cigarettes analyzed in a week or so. I may even mention that to him to get the discussion going."

"Great!"

"Jack, we might have solved this crime without you, but we might not have. At a minimum, it would have taken us a lot longer, and you know what happens when evidence gets stale."

"I do."

"Thanks, old buddy. Now go grab Grant and get back to the Club for a drink. I'll meet you there later if I can. I've got some business left to conduct with Mr. Forbes this evening."

"If it's okay with you, I'd like to call Katherine and tell her the news."

"You can tell her in person. I already called my wife and asked her to call Katherine and Georgia and have them meet us at the Club at nine. One way or another, I knew we were all going to want a drink tonight."

"What did you tell them was the occasion?"

"I told him that this was the 241st anniversary of the day that Captain Cook first sighted the Hawaiian Islands."

"Is it?"

"I don't know, but it sounds close enough to celebrate."

"Did they buy it?"

"No, but I also told them we'd be having drinks under the stars."

"Moonlight cocktails."

"It gets them every time."

"It sure does."

EPILOGUE

Peter Dillingham was beside himself on Monday afternoon as he directed guests to their tables around the Mai Tai Bar on the lanai at the Royal Hawaiian Hotel. He was, at the same time, checking with the technicians who were testing the radio broadcasting equipment and internet connection, listening to the musicians who were tuning their slack guitars and ukuleles, and giving directions to the Hawaiian dancers who would perform a hula for everyone in the Mai Tai Bar. When he saw Jack and Katherine arrive, he breathed a sigh of relief.

"Am I ever glad to see you two!"

"Why?" Jack asked. "We wouldn't miss this broadcast for the world."

"I know. It's Arthur Fairbanks. He's been running around, asking for you ever since he got here, thirty minutes ago I might add."

"What's he concerned about?" Jack asked.

"He's heard some of the details about the Derek Reynolds murder but he wants to get the full story from you."

Peter showed Jack and Katherine to his table directly in front of the broadcasting table where microphones, headphones, and computer monitors had been placed in preparation for the new edition of Hawaii's radio broadcast to the world. A cheer went up as they arrived, and Gordon and Georgia Grant, Arthur

Fairbanks, and Commander Tom Butler and Hypatia Adams rose to welcome the Sullivan's.

"What's all this about?" Jack asked, looking embarrassed.

"Sullivan, you are the hero of the day and probably the year," Gordon Grant announced in his inimitable style. "McNeil has spread the word all over town that you solved the mystery of Derek Reynolds' murder."

"Oh, I just helped with some technical research and follow-up stuff."

"That's not the way Dave tells it. He says that without your help, the police might not have solved this one at all."

"I seriously doubt that, Gordo."

"No, it's true," boomed the unmistakable voice of Dave McNeil, as he and his wife Nicole joined the group.

"My favorite golfing partner does not embellish, that I can state with certainty," Gordon Grant added.

"Jack, I've taken the liberty of telling a few people around town how much you helped us. I hope you don't mind," said McNeil.

"I wish you hadn't, Dave. I'd like to remain an anonymous lawyer and coffee farmer, as George Lane so graciously referred to me last night."

"Oh, Jack, I heard about that bloody remark from Sidney," said Arthur, "and she cut him to ribbons on the way home from the memorial service. I'm sure you'll get an apology the next time you see the Lane's," said Arthur. "And, by the way, Jack, Sidney also told me that she wants to have you back soon to see some new shrubs that George planted after your visit to replace the Dieffenbachia that a neighbor's dog was chewing daily, much to the detriment of his vocal cords, which have been paralyzed ever since."

"No apology is necessary. In fact, the "lawyer turned farmer" image has a certain Jeffersonian quality about it that I rather like."

"If only your Mr. Jefferson hadn't been so exuberant, you Yanks might still be enjoying the benefits of British citizenship," Arthur proclaimed.

"Thank you for that diplomatic note, Arthur. We really must get you a copy of the Declaration of Independence," Gordon replied laughing.

"You know, I think last night brought a lot of feelings to the surface," said Hypatia. "Even Jennifer admitted this morning that she should have restrained herself at the memorial for Derek."

"Well," Dave McNeil interjected, "if you want to hear about things rising to the surface, I can tell you that Lance Forbes erupted like a volcano last night when I confronted him with the evidence Jack dug up. By ten o'clock, he had told me the whole story. Talk about self-delusion, he actually thought Loretta would marry him if Derek was out of the picture. And he really thought he could pull it off. He didn't tell Loretta a thing about it."

"He certainly is a bloody odd choice for a murderer," said Arthur.

"They all are, Arthur," Dave said.

"Dave, my good man, how did he do it, I mean mechanically?" Arthur asked.

"It wasn't complicated. Kulani said that Forbes was sitting at the bar for most of the evening with his back toward the bar."

"Yes."

"Well, Forbes said he watched the waitresses and kept tabs on Derek's drinks. And the crowd was so large that Kulani sometimes had to hand him Mai Tai's to pass to waitresses who couldn't get close to the bar. One waitress yelled to Kulani that she needed a Mai Tai for Mr. Reynolds. I guess she wanted to make sure that Kulani made one of his best drinks for the guest of honor. Kulani handed the drink to Lance, and Lance kept it and passed the Mai Tai in his other hand, which he had already laced with 'Akia, to the waitress. With the crowd and the noise from conversation and music, no one noticed. It was that simple."

"How did he mix the poison with the Mai Tai without anyone seeing him?" Arthur asked.

"Believe it or not, he took a Mai Tai into the Men's Room, went into a stall and sat down, and then poured the poison from a small bottle he had in his pocket," Dave explained.

"That's probably what Rich Stanley heard," Jack added.

"I'll bet it was," Katherine agreed.

"But how did Forbes know he'd have that kind of opportunity?" Arthur asked.

"He didn't. He just thought he might have a chance at the party and decided he would take it if he got it. If the opportunity hadn't come up the way it did, he'd have waited for another occasion."

"I'd forgotten how banal so many crimes are," Jack said.

"But why did he run Kulani off the road? Did he think Kulani knew what he'd done?" Arthur asked.

"This guy is not an experienced criminal, and this was his first leap into the underworld. He got very scared afterwards and decided to make sure that the one man who knew he'd been at the bar all night, near the drinks while they were being made, and who had also seen him handling some of them, wouldn't be available to identify him. Fortunately for Kulani, and for us, he wasn't successful."

Arthur Fairbanks then turned to Jack and asked,

"How did you untwist it all, Jack? Did you have any other suspects?"

"I did, Arthur, each of whom had motive, means and opportunity, but the more I learned about Derek, the more I learned about Lance. I guess I just got lucky."

With that, Gordon Grant stood up and raised his glass in a toast.

"To Jack Sullivan, my lawyer, the newest coffee farmer in the Sandwich Islands, and a damn good detective."

The entire table toasted Jack, and he responded with an obvious blush. Then he stood up himself to offer a toast.

"To the most wonderful group of friends two émigrés from the east coast could ever hope to find. And to these beautiful islands, that will always hold mysteries it will be a pleasure to solve."

As they raised their glasses in response to Jack's toast, the mellifluous tones of Peter Dillingham's voice floated over their table as he spoke into the microphone.

"Good Evening, Ladies and Gentlemen around the globe, 'This Is Hawaii,' and we are broadcasting to the world from the Mai Tai Bar at the Royal Hawaiian Hotel on Honolulu's beautiful Waikiki Beach."

Jack looked at Katherine, drew her toward him, kissed her, and whispered quietly in her ear.

"I knew we were going to like it here."

"So did I," she whispered as she pulled him closer.

THE END

www.ingramcontent.com/pod-product-compliance
Lightning Source LLC
Chambersburg PA
CBHW072228170626
46813CB00003B/1136